THE DEVIL'S DAUGHTER

By Danielle Steel

The Devil's Daughter • The Colour of Hope • The Portrait • For Richer for Poorer • A Mother's Love
A Mind of Her Own • Far from Home • Never Say Never • Trial by Fire • Triangle
Joy • Resurrection • Only the Brave • Never Too Late • Upside Down
The Ball at Versailles • Second Act • Happiness • Palazzo • The Wedding Planner
Worthy Opponents • Without a Trace • The Whittiers • The High Notes • The Challenge
Suspects • Beautiful • High Stakes • Invisible • Flying Angels • The Butler • Complications
Nine Lives • Finding Ashley • The Affair • Neighbours • All That Glitters • Royal
Daddy's Girls • The Wedding Dress • The Numbers Game • Moral Compass • Spy
Child's Play • The Dark Side • Lost and Found • Blessing in Disguise • Silent Night
Turning Point • Beauchamp Hall • In His Father's Footsteps • The Good Fight • The Cast
Accidental Heroes • Fall from Grace • Past Perfect • Fairytale • The Right Time
The Duchess • Against All Odds • Dangerous Games • The Mistress • The Award
Rushing Waters • Magic • The Apartment • Property of a Noblewoman • Blue
Precious Gifts • Undercover • Country • Prodigal Son • Pegasus • A Perfect Life
Power Play • Winners • First Sight • Until the End of Time • The Sins of the Mother
Friends Forever • Betrayal • Hotel Vendôme • Happy Birthday • 44 Charles Street • Legacy
Family Ties • Big Girl • Southern Lights • Matters of the Heart • One Day at a Time
A Good Woman • Rogue • Honor Thyself • Amazing Grace • Bungalow 2 • Sisters
H.R.H. • Coming Out • The House • Toxic Bachelors • Miracle • Impossible • Echoes
Second Chance • Ransom • Safe Harbour • Johnny Angel • Dating Game
Answered Prayers • Sunset in St. Tropez • The Cottage • The Kiss • Leap of Faith
Lone Eagle • Journey • The House on Hope Street • The Wedding • Irresistible Forces
Granny Dan • Bittersweet • Mirror Image • The Klone and I • The Long Road Home
The Ghost • Special Delivery • The Ranch • Silent Honor • Malice • Five Days in Paris
Lightning • Wings • The Gift • Accident • Vanished • Mixed Blessings • Jewels
No Greater Love • Heartbeat • Message from Nam • Daddy • Star • Zoya • Kaleidoscope
Fine Things • Wanderlust • Secrets • Family Album • Full Circle • Changes
Thurston House • Crossings • Once in a Lifetime • A Perfect Stranger • Remembrance
Palomino • Love: *Poems* • The Ring • Loving • To Love Again • Summer's End
Season of Passion • The Promise • Now and Forever • Passion's Promise • Going Home

Nonfiction
Expect a Miracle
Pure Joy: *The Dogs We Love*
A Gift of Hope: *Helping the Homeless*
His Bright Light: *The Story of Nick Traina*

For Children
Pretty Minnie in Hollywood
Pretty Minnie in Paris

Danielle Steel

THE DEVIL'S DAUGHTER

MACMILLAN

First published 2026 by Delacorte Press
an imprint of Random House
a division of Penguin Random House LLC, New York

First published in the UK 2026 by Macmillan
an imprint of Pan Macmillan
The Smithson, 6 Briset Street, London EC1M 5NR
EU representative: Macmillan Publishers Ireland Limited, 1st Floor,
The Liffey Trust Centre, 117–126 Sheriff Street Upper,
Dublin 1 D01 YC43
Associated companies throughout the world

ISBN 978-1-5290-8610-2 HB
ISBN 978-1-5290-8611-9 TPB

1 3 5 7 9 8 6 4 2

A CIP catalogue record for this book is available from the British Library.

Typeset in Charter ITC by Palimpsest Book Production Ltd, Falkirk, Stirlingshire
Printed and bound in the UK using 100% Renewable Electricity by CPI Group (UK) Ltd

Visit **www.panmacmillan.com** to read more about all our books
and to buy them.

To my beloved children,

Beatrix, Trevor, Todd, Nick, Samantha,

   Victoria, Vanessa, Maxx, and Zara,

May you always be safe from the evil in the world,

love with your whole soul,

give with your whole heart,

may you be surrounded by people who love you,

and spot the bad ones quickly.

May the people you love love you well in return,

sing, dance, fly, laugh, and love to the fullest,

as I love you

with all my heart,

                                        Mom/d.s.

THE DEVIL'S DAUGHTER

Chapter 1

Wilhelmina "Billie" Banks stood looking in the mirror in her dorm room at the Massachusetts Institute of Technology in Cambridge, Massachusetts, just outside Boston. She was wearing her cap and gown, a pair of high heels she had bought for the occasion, the only ones she owned, and a serious expression. She felt as though her life was beginning at that moment. In a few minutes, she would be graduating with her class, *magna cum laude*. Without the heels, she stood just over five feet, had a slim figure and delicate features, straight dark hair, and green eyes. Even with the heels and cap and gown, she still looked like a little girl. Growing up, it had always frustrated her that people mistook her for a child at times, especially when she was in jeans and running shoes, with her hair in braids.

Today she was wearing her hair in a neat ponytail under her mortarboard with the tassel. She wished that her mother could see her, but she had died when Billie was seventeen, in her senior year of high school, the year before she had come to MIT. She still missed her terribly, especially at times like this. This was the most important moment of her life.

Billie's mother, Virginia Banks, was the only person in Billie's life who didn't think she was a freak. Virginia had been passionate about education, and learning whatever you could. Billie had majored in biology and minored in chemistry, and was a gifted science student. She had come to MIT on a full scholarship thanks to her high school counselor Virgil White, who had encouraged her to apply. He wrote the letter that got her into MIT and got her the scholarship, which had changed her life.

Billie had grown up on her father's modest dairy farm in Collins, Iowa, with a population of just under five hundred people, northeast of Des Moines. She'd done her chores every day, tending to the cows and helping her father, and then she would study late into the night. Neither of her parents had gone to college, but her mother had taught her that education was everything, even though she herself had married right out of high school and had Billie ten months later. Virginia was thirty-six when she died of breast cancer, but she was a wise, intelligent woman, who had educated herself and her oldest daughter by reading voraciously. Virginia had a passion for French literature, and had always encouraged Billie's love of science. Billie would have liked to go to medical school but she knew they couldn't afford it, and she doubted that she could get a full scholarship. She wanted to get a good job now, with a major pharmaceutical company, preferably in research. She had taken summer jobs in local laboratories in Boston, and she worked at the campus bookstore all year long for extra money. She usually spent it on books for herself. When she packed up her things from her dorm room, she had sent several boxes of books home, and hoped her father wouldn't throw them away. She was taking two boxes of books with her to the student hotel where she was moving that afternoon. She could only afford to stay there for a month at most, until she found a job. She had been studying so intently in the final months of school that she hadn't taken time to look for a job, so she was eager to find one soon. She would take almost any lab job if she had to as an interim stopgap, but she was hoping to find one in the research department at one of the big pharmaceutical companies. Her Bachelor of Science diploma from MIT was sure to get her a good position. She was planning to go to several employment agencies the Monday after graduation.

When she looked in the mirror, wearing her cap and gown, she saw the same familiar face, but she felt completely different. She suddenly felt more grown-up. She'd gotten her dark hair blown out for the occasion, and it gleamed in the neat ponytail. She hoped she looked mature enough to find a good job. She had lived by her mother's golden rule, "Education is everything," a theory her father didn't adhere to. He thought education was useless, especially for a girl. He hoped his daughters would find husbands, preferably farmers in neighboring towns, and stay near home. He had great hopes for Billie's younger sister, Michaela. Mickie was a strikingly beautiful girl, worthy of the son of any of the big farm owners nearby. Mickie was a rare beauty and the apple of her father's eye.

Their nicknames were in lieu of the sons he didn't have. Mickie was tall and blonde, and looked like him. Jim Banks was a handsome man, and she was his pride and joy. He had been born and raised in Collins, his father had built the dairy, and Jim had worked there all his life. Mickie had as little interest in education as he did and she relied on her looks and charm and artful ways to get whatever she wanted, particularly from her father. She knew just how to work him. He hung on her every word, believed everything she said, and lived to make her happy. She was three years younger than Billie, and had been fourteen when their mother died. Billie had done the best she could to mother Mickie during her final year at home, before she left for MIT, but their relationship had never been easy. Unlike Billie, Mickie looked like she was in her twenties when she was fourteen. She was fully a woman, with a spectacular figure. Men all over the county had been noticing her for years, and she'd been boy-crazy since she was thirteen. She'd been nearly impossible to control and Billie fought with her constantly when she entered high school during Billie's last year at home. She climbed out windows and went to parties at the town hall or other kids' homes. She was full of life and exuberance, constantly in trouble of some kind but always managing to get out of it. She usually blamed Billie for something she had done, and their father believed her. Most of the time Billie wound up getting punished for her sister's crimes, which Mickie thought was funny. She had no conscience at all about it and somehow Billie always let her get away with it. Their mother was wise to Mickie's ways, and could usually guess when Mickie was lying, but once their mother was gone, Billie felt an obligation to protect her sister.

The worst thing Mickie had ever done was steal their father's truck and run over the dog he loved, killing it, while she was trying to sneak out to a school dance in the next town. She ran over it and kept on driving and went to the dance. Jim Banks had been heartbroken over the dog when he found him in the morning, and Mickie said she had seen Billie do it. Billie didn't think her father had ever forgiven her. But she didn't think he liked her much anyway. He thought her fascination with science was weird, and unsuitable for a girl. Billie did all the chores at the dairy that Mickie took credit for. He never hid the fact that Mickie was his favorite from the time she was born. He paid no attention to Billie at all, except to punish her for whatever Mickie blamed on her.

Mickie had been a beautiful baby with golden curls and big blue eyes, and she had her father wrapped around her finger ever since she could talk. Billie knew better than anyone that her little sister had been lying all her life. She never hesitated to sacrifice Billie to get what she wanted. The lies she told were totally credible, with those big blue eyes and the face of an angel. Her lack of empathy for anyone else had always worried their mother. Virginia was Billie's only defender.

Everything was all about Mickie and whatever her goal was on any given day. She loved clothes and boys and dancing and going out and having fun. She teased the boys mercilessly and half the boys in their school were in love with her, and didn't mind how badly she treated them. She taunted them, and was a proficient flirt. She knew just how to drive men crazy even at twelve and thirteen, and by fourteen she was really good at it. Boys would come to visit her and they'd disappear, somewhere on the farm. Billie could guess what they were doing. Mickie drove all the boys crazy with desire for her.

After their mother died, Billie found Mickie with the captain of the basketball team where they kept the fresh hay. Billie scolded her for it afterward, and worried about her getting pregnant, and later Billie found the contraceptive pills Mickie had been given by a birth control clinic. When Billie confronted her with them, she said she'd used a fake ID that said she was eighteen, even though she was just fourteen then. But at least she never got pregnant. Billie could only imagine the heyday Mickie must have had once she had left for MIT, and from then on. Their father never tried to control her. There was no stopping her, especially when a boy was involved, and none of them could resist her. She was too beautiful and too sexy.

Boys never looked twice at Billie, even in high school. She was small and skinny and had no figure to speak of. The two girls didn't even look related, except that they each looked like one of their parents, who looked nothing alike. Virginia had been small, delicate, and graceful, like her eldest daughter. Mickie was tall, slim, and blonde like her father. She was the brightest star in the county, and Billie was the smartest, at the top of every class. That's what got her to MIT, which was just the escape she wanted.

Mickie was the prom queen every year in high school, and had managed to go to the prom even as a freshman. She had convinced the proctor that she was a year older than she was, and that there was a mistake on her student ID card. The proctor was an assistant teacher, only a year out of college herself, and no match for Mickie, who could charm anyone, especially a man, into doing what she wanted.

Billie had only gone to the prom once, junior year, with her best friend, not a boyfriend, Tom Carter. It was his senior prom. He left for West Point the year before Billie went to MIT. She missed him terribly once he'd left. They'd been best friends since grade school. They shared their hopes and dreams and secrets. He was third-generation West Point. His grandfather was a colonel. Tom went into military intelligence when he graduated. He had majored in political science, and was currently somewhere in the Middle East, at an intense antiterrorist training camp where he was taking advanced classes for two months. He had told Billie that he loved working in military intelligence. He felt like he could really make a difference there. She didn't know where he was now. He wasn't allowed to tell her. Once in a while, she got a letter from him, when he had a break and was on leave in a neutral place. He had visited her often while he was at West Point, and she had gone to his commencement. He would have been at hers if he'd been in the States.

Her father and sister didn't come to her commencement, which wasn't a surprise. They couldn't afford to. The dairy was being run on a shoestring. They'd had a couple of bad years. Her father had been sick for a while the year before, and he couldn't afford good help. He drank more than he used to when his wife was alive. He was lonely. There were no single women around on the neighboring farms. He hadn't had a girlfriend in a few years, and was no longer trying to find one. No one measured up to Virginia. She had been patient and kind, a wonderful wife and mother, and she had put up with his cold, unaffectionate ways. No other woman would have.

Billie hardly came home anymore. She'd been too busy with papers and exams during her senior year. She came back for Christmas every year and she worked at the campus bookshop all summer. Once a year in Iowa was enough. It was too depressing going back there. Her father still treated her like a misfit, which to him she was. He thought she'd gotten even stranger at MIT, being with others like her. He didn't see that she was thriving and comfortable among her peers at last. Coming back to the farm was a step back into painful history for her, a whole town of people who thought her odd, a sister who had tormented her, and their mother gone. Their father lashed out at her when he was drunk, which was every night when she was home.

Mickie had dropped out of high school a few months before graduation the year before, gotten her GED, and gone to L.A. to act in bit parts and model, mostly in trade shows, which paid well and helped manage her share of the rent in an apartment with two other girls. They all waited on tables at night at restaurants nearby, and she had told her father she was going to make it big in L.A. You couldn't keep a girl like Mickie on a farm in a small town in Iowa. She was destined for a bigger world and had thirsted for it all her life. She used to steal movie magazines and fashion magazines from the local store, and planted them in Billie's room so she'd get blamed for it. Billie didn't care about movies or fashion. She dressed in T-shirts and jeans all through high school. Her mother had known who took the magazines and would take them back to the store when she found them. But the images Mickie saw in them had marked her forever. She taught herself to do her makeup like the models, and imitated their hair. She lightened hers even more, which made her look glamorous, and she spent every penny she could on secondhand clothes that made her look sexy and stylish. Billie had seen her last on Christmas, and she was wearing a short hot pink dress that clung to her amazing figure, and six-inch heels with red soles that she said were the brand worn on *The Real Housewives of Beverly Hills* on TV. She looked totally out of place in her hometown, and like a movie star. She made Billie feel more out of place than ever.

Their father was bursting with pride when she wore a sexy fake leopard coat to church on Christmas Eve. Billie felt more like a freak and looked like Little Orphan Annie in an old down jacket of her mother's that was too big for her, but that she wore out of sentiment. It still smelled faintly of the soap Virginia had used. People looked right past Billie as they stared at Mickie. She thrived on the attention, and flirted with the boys she had gone to school with, some of whom were married by then. Their wives and girlfriends didn't appreciate the attention she lavished on them. They didn't bother talking to Billie. She'd been gone for four years by then, and her only close friend had been Tom.

The "cool girls" in school had been mean to Billie when they were younger and eventually dismissed her as just too weird. Only a few of them had gone to the state college. Most had stayed on their farms and gotten married as soon as they graduated from high school. When Billie went home, she was shocked by how many of them had children. In an entirely different way, Mickie was as big a freak as she was and didn't fit. She just looked better in her expensive secondhand wardrobe, and the other girls envied her. More than ever now, since she was single and free and lived in L.A. She had the life they wished they had but didn't have the courage, the looks, or the means to go after. The education Billie had gotten was of no interest to them, and she looked no different than she had in school. Mickie was the epitome of glamour, and had escaped their fate. It was always a relief to Billie when she left and went back to Boston, to the world where she was comfortable and fit in.

She hadn't expected her father or Mickie to come to her graduation. MIT was on another planet for them. But she wished her mother could have been there and seen her. Mickie would have laughed at her in her cap and gown, and her father hadn't worn a suit since her mother died. He wore his work clothes and rubber boots at the dairy.

Billie took a last look in the mirror and left her dorm room to hurry down the stairs to line up for the ceremony. The graduates were lining up in alphabetical order so she was close to the front of the line. She glimpsed familiar faces in the crowd and smiled and nodded. It felt bittersweet knowing that after today, she wouldn't see them again, even though she had no close friends there. She had dated a few of the men, but hadn't had a serious romance.

She'd been too busy studying and getting good grades. She'd lost her virginity her senior year, on a drunken night with her chemistry partner. It hadn't been love, just beer. He was a virgin too. They dated a few times afterward, and slowly slipped away from each other. It just seemed awkward and not romantic. It was a rite of passage and nothing more. She saw him from a distance a few times after their class together ended, and they never spoke again. His last name was Ziegler and he was the last one in the lineup for graduation. They nodded to each other as she walked past to take her place.

She assumed that everyone had family or friends there for the commencement, and thought she was the only one who didn't, but she didn't feel lonely or out of place. MIT had been her home for four years now, and she was far more at ease there than she was on the farm where she grew up. Most of the students at MIT were like her. In her hometown, she was unique.

She took her seat with her classmates, and walked onto the stage when her turn came to accept her diploma, which was a symbolic one. The real one would be sent in the mail. She shook hands with the dean of students, had her picture taken, and went back to her seat, beaming with pride as her name was read from the list of honors as *magna cum laude*. The commencement speech was given by a senator.

Billie threw her mortarboard in the air with the others, after shifting the tassel once she was officially a graduate, and was filing out, still smiling with a feeling of victory, when a boy she knew from her physics class stopped her. They weren't close but had studied together a few times. He was from Atlanta, and his parents and two sisters were standing near him when he stopped her.

"Congratulations, Billie," he said.

"Thanks, you too, Ben. Good luck." He had noticed that she was alone, and wasn't looking for anyone in the crowd. The others were all joining up with their families.

"Do you want to come to lunch with us at Harvest?" he said, waving vaguely at his family. "My grandma got sick and couldn't come. We have an extra seat at the table." He was so nice about it that she was taken by surprise and didn't know what to say.

"I . . . uh . . . your family won't mind?" She felt warm and friendly toward everyone. There was suddenly a feeling of camaraderie among them, as people hugged and said goodbye.

"They'd love it." He smiled at her.

"Okay, thank you very much." His name was Ben Hewitt, and he introduced her to his parents and his two older sisters, and all of them were pleasant and welcoming to her. He had asked their permission first and they felt bad that she was alone, as Ben did, and they told him to ask her. She followed them out to the parking area, enjoying being part of a family suddenly. One of his sisters was asking about her major. She was in med school at Georgetown, and his other sister was working in New York. They made Billie feel at home on the drive to the restaurant, and by the time they got there, she felt at ease with all of them, and had a lovely time at lunch. It was after three by the time they left the restaurant, and she thanked them, and said she had to get back to the dorm to move to the hotel. She had to be out by five. The Hewitts had made it a special day for her. She had planned to go back to her room after the ceremony and skip lunch, since she had no one to be with, and they had changed everything for her. Ben's mother hugged her when they said goodbye and wished her luck, and said to call and come visit if she ever came to Atlanta. She had the accent of the Deep South and Billie was grateful for how kind they had been to her.

"Thanks, Ben," she said, and he hugged her too. "That was really nice of you, and your family."

"It's a big day. What are you going to do now?" he asked her. "You heard the senator today, tomorrow is the first day of our adult lives."

"I'm looking for a job. I want to try to stay here in Boston." He had said he was going back to Atlanta for the summer, and then he was coming back to MIT for graduate studies in engineering.

"Maybe we can get together when I come back in the fall," he said with a smile, wondering why he had never gone out with her. She was very small and graceful, pretty and very smart. He'd had a girlfriend until a few months before, and now he was free. "I still have your number. I'll call you when I get back in August," he promised, and she wondered if he would.

"I hope I find a job so I can stay in Boston. I love it here," she said.

"Me too. We're going to Aspen in July. Are you going home?" She shook her head and didn't bother to explain. There was nothing to go home to except her father, drunk at night, pretending she didn't exist and making her feel weird, and a barn full of cows, in a town where she had lived all her life and never fit in. MIT was home now, and hopefully Boston and a job.

"I'll be working," she said, hoping it would be true. If not, she might have to go home. She had about a month's worth of money saved up from her job at the bookstore. It would run out pretty fast. Ben's family looked as though they had money. His mother and sisters were well dressed, his father was wearing a nice suit. They owned fast-food franchises all over Georgia—McDonald's and Pizza Hut, she had learned at lunch. Ben had never mentioned it before. He was a nice boy, and she hoped she'd see him again.

She went back to her dorm room after they left, changed back into jeans and a sweater, folded her dress into her only suitcase and closed it, and looked around the room to make sure she hadn't forgotten anything. She had a framed photograph of her mother in her suitcase, and none of her father or Mickie.

She knew how proud her mother would have been on that day. The Hewitts had been so nice to include her in their celebration of Ben, and he'd been kind to her too.

She carried her two boxes down the stairs one by one, took a last look around the room that had been home, and carried her suitcase down the stairs. She saw familiar faces leaving the dorm, but no one she knew well. Some of the girls were crying as they said goodbye to each other. Billie's Uber came a few minutes later, the driver loaded her boxes and suitcase into the trunk, and she gave him the address of the student hotel. As they drove off the campus, she looked at the familiar sights that had been her home for four years, and felt half excited and half scared. She remembered how terrified she had been when she arrived, afraid she wouldn't measure up. They had been the best four years of her life.

"Graduated today?" the driver asked her with a smile, and she nodded.

"Yes, I did," she said, smiling, and wiped a tear from her cheek.

"Congratulations! That's a big day. It's a great school." She nodded again, as they drove off the campus. It felt like flying suddenly, and she realized when he said it that she hadn't heard from her father or Mickie. They probably didn't even remember what day this was for her. One day seemed like the next on the farm, and Mickie was probably having fun in L.A. But Billie knew that she would remember this day for the rest of her life, every detail. She was a grown-up now, and no longer a freak. She was a graduate of MIT. She had done it, and no one could ever take this accomplishment away from her, or this day. It was the best day of her whole life.

Chapter 2

Billie spent Sunday getting organized at the hotel, and making lists of the employment agencies that serviced the Boston area. She was going to call them on Monday. She focused on the ones that had experience in the medical field, since that was where her skills and degree applied. She wanted to find a job at a laboratory, preferably in research. She went for a walk on Sunday afternoon, thinking about Ben Hewitt and his family and how nice they had been to her, and how normal they seemed. She wished she had a family like that. She might have, if her mother had lived. Virginia would have forced her father to be at least slightly more attentive, whatever his preferences for Mickie were. And she would have made Mickie behave better than she did. Now all three of them had separate lives and went their own ways. They made no effort to stay connected. She and Mickie never spoke on the phone. Once in a while they texted. Her mother would have come to her graduation even if no one else did. Her father wouldn't have, he never left the farm.

Billie wondered what it felt like to have a real family of people who cared about each other and showed up when it mattered. The last five years since her mother's death had dissolved all remnants of the glue that had held them together. She felt like an orphan sometimes. She was closer to her friend Tom than to her father and sister. And now she couldn't even communicate with him, since he was on secret missions for the U.S. Army, working underground on counterterrorism. She didn't know where he was, but surely it was someplace dangerous. Every few months he'd surface and call her. She missed the days when they were in school together and saw each other every day. He had left for West Point when her mother died, so she had lost both of the people she loved at once, and was left with a sister who cared about no one but herself, and a father who had ignored her for her entire life. It wasn't much to hold on to. But she couldn't think about that now. She had to focus on finding a job.

She called all three employment agencies on Monday morning and made appointments to see two of them that afternoon and one the next day. When she got there, they told her that the new graduates had snatched up all the jobs months before, anticipating their entry into the workforce, and it was slim pickings now as a result. She was coming late to the party, and they had nothing for her. She filled out all the forms and was willing to take a temporary job in the meantime. There was occasional relief work in the labs at Mass General, but not at the moment. Billie was discouraged when she went back to the hotel that afternoon. She started looking for jobs online, and found nothing there either. She scoured the newspaper and called the agencies back for the next two weeks, and didn't get a single interview. The agencies were flooded with the latecomers like her, who had done nothing about finding a job until after graduation. The market was glutted with young people looking for work, and all the good jobs were gone.

Trying not to panic, she decided to go to New York for a few days, to see what she could turn up there. She was beginning to worry she'd run out of money. The campus bookstore gave her a few days' work, but it was slow season for them, and they couldn't give her a full-time job, just some shifts to fill in. But New York was a big city and there would be more opportunities. She took the train to New York, and stayed at a youth hostel on the Lower East Side. She made the rounds of the major hospitals, to see if she could get some relief work at their labs, but they were fully staffed with regular personnel and summer interns who had lined up jobs months before. It was hard to believe that in a city the size of New York, she couldn't find a single job.

She had ten days of money left when she got back to Boston, and touched base with the agencies again, to no avail. She was sitting on a park bench, considering what to do next. If all else failed and she couldn't find employment, she'd have no choice but to go back to Iowa and help her father at the farm, until she could find a job somewhere, maybe in Des Moines, or even Chicago. She didn't want to go back to the Midwest. She hated the bitter winters, and she loved Boston. But she couldn't stay there without a job, and she couldn't afford the hotel for much longer. She was angry at herself for not having looked for a job months before, but she had been finishing her papers and focusing on her exams, and hadn't had the time to job hunt. She kept putting it off, and now it was too late.

She was on the verge of tears when her phone rang, and she was surprised to see from the caller ID that it was Mickie. She never called unless she wanted something, and there was nothing Billie could do for her. She answered the call, and Mickie sounded bright and cheerful, but Billie knew that something was up if she was calling. She wondered if something had happened to their father. He was only forty-one, but he was aging prematurely. The life of a farmer wasn't easy, and his drinking didn't help. He looked sixty when Billie had seen him at Christmas.

"Hi, Mick. What's up? Is Dad okay?" Billie said when she answered.

"I don't know. Why? Has he been sick? I haven't talked to him in a couple of months." Neither had Billie. It reminded her again of how disconnected they were. They were hardly even a family anymore, as her graduation had demonstrated.

"I just wondered if that was why you were calling," Billie said, trying not to sound as down as she was.

"No. When are you graduating?" Mickie asked, and Billie knew there had to be a reason for the question.

"Three weeks ago. Why?"

"Oh. Sorry I missed it. I thought it was in June." It had always been May, but it wasn't on Michaela's radar since it wasn't about her. "Where are you?"

"I'm in Boston."

"Are you working?"

"Not yet. I'm looking for a job."

"Why don't you come to L.A., and look for one here?" Los Angeles seemed like it was part of another universe to Billie. She had never been to California, but Mickie seemed to love it, the weather, the people, the modeling opportunities. She loved being in a big, spread-out city, with so much going on. She couldn't imagine living anywhere else now, and going back to Iowa would be like a prison sentence.

"It's a long way to go, and I don't know anyone, except you."

"You could stay with me. You could even wait tables where I work. They're always hiring extra girls to fill in on the weekends. It's good money and the tips are great." It wasn't like Mickie to make helpful suggestions unless they helped her too. Billie could smell an agenda in there somewhere, she just didn't know what it was yet.

"What's happening with you?" Billie asked her. L.A. seemed so far away, and she wasn't eager to live with Mickie. Somehow Billie always ended up getting the short side of any deal that involved her sister.

Mickie was more direct than usual. "I just lost both my roommates. One moved in with her boyfriend and left me high and dry on a day's notice, and the other one is moving back to Dallas. Her dad is sick and her mom is paying for her to go home. I have a great apartment. I love it, and I don't know anyone who's looking for a place right now. I can't afford it on my own. But maybe if you get a decent job, we could split it between the two of us. I just wondered if you'd be interested. Hell, Billie, why don't you come out here and give it a shot? The weather is better than Boston, and it's a lot more fun." There were over two hundred thousand students in Boston, which had made it young and lively for Billie for four years, but now she couldn't find a job. Los Angeles was on the other side of the country, and she was leery of moving in with her sister. She knew what that was like. She wondered if Mickie had grown up enough to make it possible. She was nineteen and had been in L.A. for more than a year, and she'd had roommates, which must have taught her something about not running roughshod over other humans. Billie didn't want to relive what it had been like living with her growing up, but they were both adults now, so maybe it could work.

"I'm not sure I have enough money to spare for a ticket to L.A.," Billie said cautiously, "and if I don't find a job there, I will be flat broke and won't have enough to even get back to Iowa."

"I'll lend it to you if that happens," Mickie said confidently. She made good money on tips at the restaurant where she worked, and there were plenty of trade shows in L.A. where she got modeling jobs. They didn't pay a lot but they covered her rent, if she had a roommate to pay the other half.

"How much would my share of the rent be?" Billie asked her. Mickie told her, and it would be impossible for her without a job. Pretty soon dinner would be impossible without a job. Her situation was going to be desperate soon. Flying to L.A. would really drain what she had left. But there didn't seem to be any jobs for her in Boston. It was a tough call. She could get a waitress job in Boston, but the labs and employment agencies hadn't held out any hope of a real job anytime soon.

"I'll ask the manager at the restaurant if he can give you work until you find a job," Mickie said soothingly. "And see if you can get a cheap seat to L.A. online. You can always find a deal. I'll call you later."

Billie didn't know what to do, so she took Mickie's advice and checked on the internet. She found a ticket on a red-eye that made two stops crossing the country and was surprisingly cheap. She had enough money to pay for it, but it would leave her very little once she got to California. She would have to take the waitressing job or whatever else she could get while she combed the employment agencies for a real job. She hated to give up on Boston, but she couldn't afford to hold out much longer, and with Mickie, she'd have a roof over her head. In Boston very shortly she wouldn't even have that. Feeling very anxious, she bought the ticket online, and notified the hotel that she was leaving that night. Her three-week job hunt had been futile. She never would have thought that she'd be going to Los Angeles to live with her sister. But there was no one for her to lie to now, or to blame Billie for things she hadn't done. They were two grown women who would be living with each other. She just hoped that her sister was mature enough now to handle it like an adult, and not the little monster she'd been when they were growing up. She assumed that life on her own for the past year and a half, and with roommates, would have taught her something. It never dawned on Billie that Mickie might have lost her roommates for other reasons. She believed her. Mickie was always so convincing. In a single phone call, in a matter of minutes, she had convinced Billie to leave Boston, and move to L.A. to live with her.

Mickie called her back from work at the restaurant, right before Billie left the hotel, and told her that her manager had promised to give Billie night shifts at the restaurant for a couple of weeks, since some of the waitresses were taking vacation, and he could use the help. And if he liked her style, he might offer her a regular job, which Mickie said she could use to supplement her income, even if she found a day job. Billie hoped she wouldn't need to do that, if she found a job she was qualified for with her degree from MIT. Mickie was a high school dropout, and she was in better financial shape than Billie. It would have proved their father right if he'd known. Fortunately, he didn't. Neither of them ever talked to him, and he didn't call them. Billie hoped her dire situation was only temporary. It was terrifying, no longer having the scholarship to depend on, no other source of income, and watching her meager savings dwindle day by day. She felt incredibly stupid not having dealt with it by lining up a job long before graduation.

Mickie gave her the address of the apartment when she called, and Billie thanked her for getting her the job at the restaurant. She told her when she was arriving. Her flight was leaving Boston at midnight, and zigzagging across the country, with a stop in Chicago, and another in Phoenix. She was due to land in L.A. at eleven A.M. local time after two long layovers. She'd be traveling for fourteen hours to get there, but the ticket was dirt cheap.

When she got to the airport, she checked her two boxes of books. She didn't have time to ship them to Iowa that day, and they were her favorites, textbooks she wanted to be able to refer to if she got a job in a research lab, to refresh her memory if she needed to. She checked her suitcase with them, and hoped it would all arrive in L.A. without getting lost on the way. She was wearing jeans and an MIT sweatshirt, and running shoes with holes in them. She had her hair in braids and wasn't wearing any makeup, and looked like a kid going to camp. The woman at the airline counter took a good look at her to make sure she was old enough to be traveling alone.

The economy seats were so close together on the flight,

she couldn't put her seat back at all. No food was served and she was too nervous to eat anyway. She hoped that everything would work out, and that moving in with Mickie wouldn't be a mistake. She never would have guessed that she'd do something like this, but she had no other options at the moment. She was going to do everything she could to get a lab job in L.A., even as the lowest assistant. She hadn't spent four years at MIT in order to be a waitress and forget everything she'd learned and been trained for. She was off to a bumpy start after her moment of glory on graduation day. *Magna cum laude* hadn't done her any good so far, and she hoped she'd get lucky in L.A.

She had a five-hour layover at O'Hare in Chicago, took her backpack with her and had a cup of coffee in the airport and walked around, and then dozed in a seat in the airport for a few hours. She got back on the plane when her six A.M. flight for Phoenix was called. She fell asleep again as soon as the flight took off, and bought a breakfast wrap on the plane before they landed in Phoenix. She wandered around the airport again, and couldn't wait to get to L.A. She felt wrinkled and grungy. She splashed cold water on her face in the bathroom and re-braided her hair. A boy who looked about fifteen tried to pick her up while she waited for her flight for the last leg of the trip, his mother gave her disapproving looks, and she realized what a mess she must look like. He asked her what MIT was, and she said it was a university in Cambridge, Massachusetts.

"Cool shirt. Is it vintage?" She had washed it a million times in the last four years.

"No, it's just old." She wanted to tell him that she had just graduated from there three weeks ago, *magna cum laude,* so they'd know she was respectable, but she didn't. She finally got back on the plane for the final flight of the journey. She could have flown to Tahiti or halfway around the globe in the time it had taken her to fly from Boston to Los Angeles.

They landed on time and Billie collected her boxes and bag, grateful they had arrived with her, and took a bus into the city. From there she took an Uber to Mickie's address in West Hollywood. It had been the longest trip of her life. She felt filthy by then, and she couldn't wait to peel off her clothes and take a shower. It was hot in L.A. When the Uber dropped her off, she stood looking at a slightly shabby building with a small pool next to it. Mickie had left the keys with the building manager, who handed them to Billie. Mickie had said she had a go-see for a modeling job that day, and said she'd be home around four.

Billie carried the boxes and suitcase up the stairs to the third-floor apartment, let herself in, and almost cried with relief. There was a small, sparsely furnished living room.

The furniture was threadbare and the couch was stained. There were no curtains on the windows or pictures on the wall, and an ugly light fixture hung from the ceiling, but it looked like a palace to Billie, and for now it was home. There were three small bedrooms, one with shoes all over the floor and a bed piled high with discarded outfits Mickie had tried on for the go-see, and the other two bedrooms, which each had a bed, a chair, and a dresser. Billie dumped her belongings in one of them. She had never been so happy to be anywhere in her life. She pulled off the MIT sweatshirt and her jeans, kicked off her shoes, and lay on the bed in her underwear. There was no air-conditioning but she didn't care. The heat felt good, and after she lay there for a while, she went and took a shower and washed her hair, wrapped herself in a clean towel from a stack in the only bathroom, and walked around the small apartment. There was a tiny basic kitchen, and a small balcony. She stood on it and looked down at the pool. She felt like she was in a whole different world from the one she had left. The most illustrious universities in the country were in Cambridge, on beautiful campuses where the elite had been educated for centuries. In L.A., everything looked either new or shabby, in a funny patchwork of Spanish-style houses and modern facades with swimming pools of different shapes and sizes in every backyard. It looked like a movie set, and Billie felt like she was in one as she took her laptop out of her back-pack and turned it on, and looked up the employment agencies she needed to contact as soon as possible. A number of them specialized in medical jobs. She jotted down the names and phone numbers, and had time to call two before Mickie got home. By the time she did, Billie had two appointments for the next day. She didn't waste any time. Her situation was dire.

She heard Mickie's key turn in the lock shortly before four. By then, Billie was wearing clean jeans and a T-shirt. Her hair was wet and hanging down her back, and her feet were bare. She looked up and saw a vision enter the apartment that made it feel more than ever that she was in a movie and not real life. The tall, beautiful blonde woman standing in front of her was wearing a lavender linen Chanel suit, an expensive handbag, and six-inch high heels. Everything Mickie was wearing was easily recognizable as a luxury brand, and she had little diamond studs glimmering on her ears. She looked straight out of *Vogue,* or like the wife of a successful Beverly Hills executive who had wandered into the wrong address. Billie laughed and looked up at her sister. She looked incredible, and her makeup was flawless as she tossed her modeling portfolio onto the small dining table and grinned at Billie.

"When did you win the lottery?" Billie asked her, and

went to give her a hug. Mickie towered over her older sister in the Louboutin heels, and allowed herself to be hugged.

"I have *the* best secondhand shop in the world in Beverly Hills. There's some woman exactly my size who sends them fabulous stuff, never worn, with the labels still on, and they sell it for a fraction of what she paid for it. I have a closet full of Chanel. I buy it with my tips, and pay the rent from the trade shows," Mickie said proudly. On closer inspection, Mickie looked like the daughter of a wealthy Beverly Hills executive, in sharp contrast to Billie's student wardrobe of faded T-shirts and jeans. "How was the flight?"

"Long. All three of them," Billie said with a groan. For a minute, and for the first time, she felt as though she had a sister. Mickie looked happy to see her, and seemed relaxed. She had never looked better. She got more beautiful every day. And not seeing her very often, Billie noticed her looking even more glamorous and sophisticated than she had at Christmas. She had developed a whole new look in L.A.

"I'm glad you took that bedroom," Mickie said, noticing. "I put my clothes in the closet of the other one. I've run out of room. With just the two of us here, I was thinking of turning that whole bedroom into a closet," which meant that she'd be using two of the bedrooms, but only paying half the rent, Billie realized quickly. Mickie still thought of her own needs first, and no one else's, but she was young, and she was much nicer to Billie than the last time she'd seen her.

"I just called the employment agencies. I have two appointments tomorrow and one the day after."

"And you're coming to work with me tonight," Mickie reminded her, and shortly after changed into thigh-high black leather boots, a black leather miniskirt, and a cropped red sweater that bared her midriff. She was wearing bright red lipstick and her long blonde hair was piled on her head and held with a clip. Billie didn't say it, but she thought Mickie looked like a hooker. Billie was wearing a denim skirt with a pink halter top Mickie had lent her, and pink high-top sneakers. She wondered what the restaurant was like, and she was quiet in the Uber on the way there. Mickie had always been a lot wilder than she was. She hoped it wouldn't be a rough crowd.

As it turned out, it was a restaurant and bar called Harry's. They had Billie busing tables for her first night, clearing away the dishes. The waitresses got tips, the bus girls didn't. All of them were scantily clad, and the customers were mostly male, and loud, and heavy drinkers. But nothing inappropriate happened. There were no bar fights. There were some couples in the back. It wasn't a family restaurant, but it wasn't terrible either. Just a lot of drunk guys in downtown L.A. It wasn't the kind of place Billie enjoyed, but Mickie was at home there. Despite her delicate looks, she wasn't intimidated by a room full of men checking her out. A few asked for dates or her phone number and she ignored them. She cleaned up in tips at the end of the evening. The other girls were pleasant, but they weren't overly friendly with Billie. They were busy all night, and at two A.M., they left and had earned their money. The trays were heavy, and the bar was loud. The manager divided up the tips at the end of the evening, and the other women left quickly. Even Mickie admitted that she was tired, and she had a go-see booked the next day. Billie had the two employment agencies to go to. The two sisters said good night and went to their rooms when they got home, and all Billie could do was pray that she would find a job soon. She hadn't gone to MIT to be a waitress in a scuzzy bar in L.A. She turned off the light and fell asleep instantly, and she couldn't believe how fast morning came.

Chapter 3

B illie made coffee for both of them the next morning when she got up. There were three mugs and a few mismatched plates in the kitchen cabinet and nothing in the fridge. Mickie showed up in the kitchen before her go-see, drank a cup of coffee, and put her portfolio in the tote bag she used for work. Billie could see the bag was Chanel from the double C's embossed in the leather. Mickie was wearing a white silk Chanel jacket, jeans, and high heels. She looked elegant and demure in her daytime persona. It was dizzying how fast she could switch from one style to another. This was her daytime look going to modeling go-sees, and at night she looked like a hooker at the bar, but she didn't behave like one. Billie was impressed by how different she could look.

"What are you trying out for today?" Billie asked her, as they both drank their coffee. Billie felt like she was supposed to take care of her sister again, the way she had after their mother died. But Mickie wasn't fourteen anymore. She was every bit a woman, and she knew what she was doing, much more so than her older sister, who felt newborn next to her and was naïve.

"They told me to dress conservatively. It's for a Beverly Hills plastic surgeon. He's running an ad campaign. He moved here from Palm Beach a couple of years ago, and he's opening a fancy beauty clinic. He picked eight girls out of a hundred, and he wants to see us today. Then he'll reduce it to one for his ads."

"That sounds pretty brutal," Billie said.

"It's how it works," Mickie said, as she set the empty cup down. "He uses all non-invasive procedures. It's a revolutionary process." She was convinced of its success even before she'd met him.

"Have you seen him?" Billie asked, observing her younger sister. Her beauty was flawless.

"I'm meeting him today. Good luck at the agency," Mickie said, and flew out the door with her portfolio. Billie was surprised that she was actually enjoying being with her. Mickie lived in a world that was completely unfamiliar to Billie. A world of appearances where one was constantly judged on how one looked, and daily rejection was part of it. Just the idea sounded exhausting. Mickie had to claw her way up, start from scratch at every go-see and audition, and then work hard as a waitress all night to pay her rent. It seemed much harder than getting a job because of one's knowledge and intelligence. Billie was wearing a crisp white blouse, black jeans, and her one pair of high heels, with her hair pulled back. She thought about wearing lipstick and decided not to. She didn't want to look frivolous. She wanted to look serious and professional.

She arrived at the first agency on time, filled out all the forms, met with an older woman, and answered all her questions. They were impressed that she had gone to MIT. At the second agency, they sent her on an interview for a temporary job at Cedars-Sinai's pathology lab. She would be replacing a lab technician going on maternity leave. It was a very basic job, and Billie was capable of a great deal more than that, but she needed the money and had said she would take anything. Two other young women were interviewed for the same job and the interviewer said they'd let her know. It was a huge hospital, and Billie walked around afterward and then went back to the apartment. She wondered how Mickie's go-see had gone. It had felt good to be in a hospital setting. It was a world she understood, and where she felt safe and competent. She would have hated being judged by her looks every day. It seemed exhausting. But Mickie was excited and energetic when she got home. She said the go-see with the plastic surgeon had been fantastic. He was setting up a whole beauty center in a fabulous house in Bel Air.

"His techniques are revolutionary," she said to Billie, as she sprawled on the couch and took her Chanel jacket off. "They sent me on two more go-sees after that. And I'm booked at a trade show at the Fairplex in Pomona this weekend. I think it's the boat show. I have to show up for work in a bikini. It's for two days, so the rent will get paid this month. The doctor is a really fancy guy. Alexander Addison the Fourth. He practiced in Palm Beach, moved to L.A., and is opening his beauty center in a week or two. They're shooting his ads next week. It's a three- or four-day job. They'll use me for the 'after' photos," she said.

"After what?" Billie asked her.

"After his miracle treatments," Mickie said vaguely.

"Will he perform them on you?" Billie looked worried. Mickie was so perfectly beautiful that the idea of anyone playing with her face was frightening.

"No, they do the photos with technology," Mickie said blithely.

"What kind of technology?"

"You know, Photoshop. The photographer does it. They

don't touch me." That sounded even worse to Billie. It sounded like a scam to her.

"Does the agency check the doctor out?"

"Of course. He went to Harvard. He's a big deal in the East. He wanted to bring his talents out here. Several major actresses are already his clients."

"Just be careful," Billie warned her, skeptical about Dr. Alexander Addison IV. "Don't let anyone push you into something you don't want to do, or feel uncomfortable about."

"He's going to pay me a fortune, Billie, if I get the job. And I'm very comfortable about that." Mickie grinned at her older sister. This was how big careers were made, and a lot of money, which was what Mickie was after. She had grown up poor and hated it. She was convinced that she was born to be rich, and she was willing to do whatever she had to do to get there. Dr. Alex Addison looked like a golden ticket to the moon to her. She just hoped she'd get the job. She had met him and he was a good-looking, successful rich guy. That was good enough for her, no matter what Billie said.

They worked at the restaurant that night, and the manager let Billie wait on tables. She made a healthy amount on tips, and Mickie made four times as much. Men loved even just talking to her. They always had, even when she was a teenager.

"I'm going shopping with this wad tomorrow," Mickie said with a grin in the Uber on the way home. It had been a long, busy night, but it was well worth it. Billie was just glad to have some money to add to her dwindling savings, and she was praying she'd get the path lab job at Cedars-Sinai. She wasn't going to set the world on fire with it, but maybe she'd learn something from the practical experience. It was a steady income, and she wouldn't have to wait on tables half naked, looking like a chorus girl in Vegas. She missed talking to Tom at times like this. He always saw the humor in things, and would make her laugh about it. Instead, she was well out of her comfort zone, and living with the sister who had been the bane of her existence for most of her childhood and adolescence. The irony of it was amusing, but Billie just wanted to retreat into her safe, familiar world, out of sight, using her brain and everything she had studied for four years.

She wondered about what Mickie was getting herself into. She had looked up Alexander Addison online and found several articles by him in respectable publications. The guy was either a genius or a brilliant charlatan, and Billie always favored the cynical, conservative point of view. She would be suspicious of him until proven wrong. But medical treatments that were related to beauty were foreign to her, and Mickie knew a lot more about them. Billie knew chemistry and science, and had won the physics prize in high school. Dr. Addison's particular brand of voodoo and witchcraft sounded like science fiction to her, but clearly his magic had worked on some people who had written rave reviews, so more power to him.

They both got lucky the next day. Mickie got the call first from her agency. She had gotten the shoot for Dr. Addison's ads. He had stretched it to four or five days. They were starting on Monday. They wanted her to bring some of her designer wardrobe, and he would provide the rest and fill in any gaps. They would be shooting at his beauty center in Bel Air, which he was calling Bellissima. It was still in the process of being decorated. They were putting the finishing touches on it. Addison was paying Mickie top dollar, and she ran around the apartment screaming and jumped up and down on the sagging couch like a little girl, while Billie grinned. The poised, sophisticated mask had slipped for a minute, and Mickie looked like a kid as she squealed and hugged her sister.

"Good job, sis," Billie said, genuinely happy for her. It was the first really big job she had landed since coming to L.A., and the agency was pleased. It would push her up to the next level of the jobs they would send her to. Success was beckoning and the doors were slowly opening, and

Mickie couldn't wait to walk through them. This was what she had come to L.A. for.

She had to go to the agency a few hours later to sign extensive confidentiality agreements that the doctor was requiring since the ads were about medical treatments. Mickie would have signed whatever he wanted.

Billie was alone in the apartment when the employment agency called her about the job at Cedars-Sinai. It was a much quieter call than Mickie's, for a lot less money. But it was security, and money she could live on. She had the job for four to six months to cover the lab tech's maternity leave. She was expecting twins and was on bed rest, and her leave might go longer, which suited Billie. She was going to be working in the pathology lab of the most prestigious hospital in L.A. The cases would be interesting. She'd be working with highly trained technicians and outstanding doctors. It was the perfect job for her. She was due to start in two days and she could hardly wait. She didn't run around the apartment screaming. She sat quietly on the couch, all alone, with a broad smile of relief on her face.

The move to California had been the right one, and she was actually enjoying getting to know her sister as the person she had grown up to be. Mickie had been fifteen when Billie left for college, and she had changed a lot in the last four years. Their paths and personalities were completely different, but the nasty little brat Mickie had been as a young teenager seemed to have metamorphosed into a somewhat interesting young woman. Billie was beginning to feel a deep-rooted affection and respect for her. It reminded her of something her father always said, and had reminded her of often when Mickie drove her crazy when they were both younger. He had told her never to forget that blood was thicker than water, and bottom line, they were sisters and that meant a lot more than friendship. Billie was beginning to discover that, and almost forgave her the trials of her childhood. Maybe they didn't really matter once you grew up. She was beginning to suspect that was the case.

She couldn't wait to tell Mickie that night that she got the job at Cedars-Sinai. It wasn't as glamorous an accomplishment as Mickie's. It wasn't glamorous at all. But it was solid and she would be able to pay her half of the rent. And it gave her time to look for an even better job while she had the safety of the long-term temp job at Cedars for the duration of someone's maternity leave. It gave her breathing space, and was exactly what she needed right now. Their prayers had been answered. Mickie had gotten the job that would push her up the ladder to greater success, and Billie had gotten the security she needed to retreat into peaceful anonymity in the pathology lab of a terrific hospital.

Mickie was happy for her too. She had come home after signing all the confidentiality agreements, with half a dozen enormous shopping bags filled with never-worn designer clothes at bargain prices. They looked as though they had been made for her, and would enhance her image whenever she went out in public wearing them, to go-sees or publicity events she might get invitations to, which was the next item on her wish list. Her face and name had to become known to achieve the fame she wanted. Celebrity meant everything to Mickie, and would have been Billie's worst nightmare. She enjoyed being invisible, and unknown. She just wanted to be part of a team that did great things in medical research. The sisters' dreams were very different, and always had been. It was hard to believe they had the same parents and had grown up in the same house.

They were both busy getting ready for their new adventures. Billie opened her boxes of books and reread the two she had on abnormal clinical pathology. She did her laundry and picked out her best T-shirts and blouses and newest jeans to wear under her lab coat. There was no dress code, and she would have no interactions with the public, only with the medical staff, but she wanted to look neat and presentable.

Mickie picked the outfits she wanted to take to the shoot,

the shoes that went with them, and some vintage Chanel costume jewelry she had bought at her favorite store. She had her hair lightened again with highlights, and bought a bottle of champagne to celebrate with Billie. Mickie was being paid twenty thousand dollars for the shoot, and she wanted to be as perfect as she could be. She had a manicure and pedicure and tried to get Billie to go with her, but Billie did her nails herself, wanted to wear them short for the lab, and didn't like wearing nail polish. Their mother hadn't worn any either.

"I must have been switched at the hospital at birth," Mickie said as they finished the champagne the night before they started their jobs. "Some glamorous movie star must have given birth in that miserable hellhole we grew up in. She left me by mistake and took the daughter who would have been happy working at the dairy for the rest of her life, and she's miserable now somewhere here in L.A., desperately searching for a cow to milk on Sunset Strip." Billie laughed. Mickie could be funny at times, usually at someone else's expense.

"Where does that leave me? How do you explain me landing in the middle of Iowa?" Billie said, and emptied the last drops in her champagne glass.

"Oh, for you, my darling older sister, our mother must have had a clandestine affair with Albert Einstein, who drove through town on a secret mission, fell in love with our mother, and nine months later, she gave birth to you, our very own little genius." They both laughed and went to their bedrooms to finish preparing for the next day.

They were both dressed when they met in the kitchen the next morning for a cup of coffee. Mickie looked exquisite in her white Chanel suit, which was her favorite, and fit her perfectly. It looked like haute couture on her, and she was wearing her fake diamond studs in her ears, and had a pair of pearl earrings in her purse.

Billie was wearing a brand-new pink T-shirt, with matching pink sneakers, her hair in a neat ponytail down her back, and a brand-new pair of Levis.

"Do you want to borrow my Chanel jeans?" Mickie asked Billie. Her sister laughed.

"They'll be two feet too long on me, and they'd probably think I stole them. They aren't going to pay me enough for Chanel jeans, but thank you anyway."

They left at the same time in two separate Ubers and wished each other luck. Mickie hadn't been to her waitress job in three days and had told them she wouldn't be in for the next week, and nor would Billie. She had only been a fill-in anyway. The restaurant rearranged Mickie's shifts. She was a good waitress and they didn't want to lose her, and they'd made adjustments for her before when she got modeling shoots. With her looks, they knew they wouldn't have her forever. They had enough unemployed actresses to draw on who were always looking for work.

Billie headed for Cedars-Sinai, and still looked like a kid going to camp. She was immaculate and tidy. She'd even pressed her jeans, but she barely looked like a grown-up. Mickie looked as though she should be riding in a limousine as the car headed for Bel Air with garment bags, two tote bags, and everything she needed for her change of outfits at the elegant house that would soon be the home of Bellissima, under the auspices of Dr. Alexander Addison IV. And he lived in an apartment upstairs.

Mickie was excited as she stepped out of the car, looking like a movie star, and the photographer the doctor had hired, Zack Campbell, snapped her picture as she was arriving. After that, he took her bags and carried them inside for her. He shot a lot of models, and was indifferent to most of them, but Mickie had caught his eye at the go-see and captured his attention from the first moment he saw her. There was something special about her. When she looked you in the eye, you felt as though you were all that mattered to her.

The doctor was waiting in the living room, which had been turned into a studio for the shoot. Zack's two assistants had lit the scene, and they were going to photograph Mickie looking relaxed and at ease in a corner of the area that would be used as a waiting room. Alex Addison loved the Chanel suit, and wanted Mickie to wear it in the first shots. A stylist went through the wardrobe Mickie had brought and approved almost all of it. A makeup artist put some finishing touches on her face, and the hairstylist brushed her long blonde hair and laid it carefully on her shoulders. They had a full crew for the five-day shoot. The photographer's assistants were already lighting the next setup.

They worked straight through until one o'clock, and did several shots in the exam rooms. The catering truck had already arrived by then and set up food for all of them in the gorgeous black granite kitchen, which was in sharp contrast to the white expanses of the house. It had been done by a well-known Italian designer. Dr. Addison had gone all out to staff the shoot adequately. Right before they stopped for lunch, Zack, Alex, and Mickie, who called herself Michaela for the shoot, went into Alex's private office, closed the door, and took the close-up headshots that were going to be the essence of his ad campaign and the centerpiece of a very expensive brochure he was having made. After he took the shots, Zack made several adjustments on his computer and had Alex watch the progression of the image closely. Mickie wasn't paying attention to what they were doing. Alex narrowed his eyes as he watched it, and then held up a hand and spoke sharply, "There! Now! Stop, back up a hair . . . perfect. You got it!" He beamed at Zack and patted him on the shoulder. Both men were the same age, forty-two, but Alex had an air of command that took over the moment he walked into a room. He had electric blue eyes, and when he and Mickie looked at each other, she swore she could hear sparks flying and feel them. He exuded a kind of mesmerizing electricity that paralyzed you for a fraction of an instant, and then energized you. She could feel it in her bones and so could he.

"You're a very special woman, Michaela," he said to her again and again. "You have powers that come from another lifetime, another world, possibly another universe."

He escorted her into the kitchen to get something to eat. They put food on their plates and he led her out the back door to a cabana by the pool with a table and chairs, where they could have privacy and eat, while the others ate in the kitchen. He talked about growing up on an estate in Southampton, living with his grandparents after his parents died in a horrible accident on their yacht. Boarding school in England after his grandparents died, undergraduate and medical school at Harvard, living and working in New York, five years of practicing in Palm Beach, and needing a more dynamic city to work in. L.A. appeared to be the perfect place, so here he was, and he told Mickie that she was part of the magic now, the destiny that controlled them all. He had no wife or children, and said he had put all his love and energy into his medical practice.

"You must think I'm crazy for saying that," he said gently, "but I felt an incredible connection to you from the first time I met you." He was mesmerizing, like a magnet she couldn't pull away from and escape, and didn't want to. He wanted to be near her and soak up her energy and combine it with his own. They lay down on the lounge chairs at the pool, waiting for one of Zack's assistants to come and get them for the rest of the shots. Zack was sure that he had already gotten some very important shots, but he sensed that there were others too.

Before they left the comfortable chairs, she asked him a direct question: "How do the treatments really work?" she asked in barely more than a whisper. She called him "Doctor," and he corrected her immediately.

"Alex," he said firmly. "The answer to your question is easy. Your skin has a memory, your body, your heart, every part of you. The chemicals I use in the injections waken the memory cells in your skin, and tell them to go back to the way they were twenty years ago, and they do what they're told. It's really as simple as that. I could look twenty now if I wanted to, but I don't want to. Those weren't the best years of my life. These are, truly helping people to look the way they feel, the way they want to be remembered and remember themselves when they meet someone now. We can achieve some amazing results, both physically and psychologically. I'm honored to be a part of it." Mickie was so taken with him and so in awe of him.

She couldn't take her eyes from his, as though they had gotten tangled up together, and his gaze on her was like an embrace.

Before they went back to the others to continue the photo shoot, Zack beckoned them both back to Alex's office. There was a light box sitting on the desk to view slides, and a computer where Alex wrote his emails and the occasional article to share his discoveries with the world. Zack had already sent the images to Alex's computer, and at a mere touch, two faces appeared on the screen. One looked vaguely familiar and the other was clearly Mickie. When you looked again, like an unsolved mystery, you saw that the first image was Mickie too. Zack had advanced it in time, and the technology allowed them to see what Mickie would look like at forty, and then a third image appeared of Michaela at forty-five. She stared at her image.

"Wow, I look like shit at forty-five," Mickie commented.

"I think maybe forty-five is too much," Alex said critically. "Forty is better." The changes in her face at forty were noticeable. She was still a ravishing woman, but her face had lost some of its definition, the spark in her eyes, the glow of her skin. It was a realistic view of Mickie in twenty years, twenty-one years, to be exact.

Alex looked across at Zack then, and nodded. "It's perfect. We got it. That's done. Freeze it," he said with an intense tone in his voice that shook Michaela to her core.

"What are you going to do with those?" she asked him innocently, and he smiled at her. She felt as though she had won the lottery when he did.

"Those are our before and after pictures," he answered simply. Mickie looked puzzled.

"Which is which?" He pointed to the digitally aged photograph of her at forty.

"That is when you first came to see me, isn't it, my dear," he said, looking deep into her eyes. "And this one," he pointed to the real one of Mickie as she looked now, "this one is after treatments. The after picture." She looked shocked for an instant, as though she was trying to compute it in her mind, and it didn't.

"It's what they will understand. And it's true, really. I could make you look twenty years younger, if I chose to, right now. But at your age that would be a bit silly, wouldn't it? They'd be looking at a newborn baby. So we fast-forward to now, and then up ahead at how you will look, and the photograph today is the after picture." He said it so smoothly that it was like watching an expert of the shell game move the shells swiftly around the table until you were no longer sure what you had seen or where the pea was.

"Is that really honest?" she asked him.

"Yes, it is. It's a projection of reality and there is nothing wrong about that. This will be very helpful to people trying to make the decision about whether to proceed with our treatments." Even Mickie knew they wouldn't look like her at nineteen, if they already looked like the older version. But somehow she wanted to believe him and broke into a broad smile.

"That's genius!" she said. He nodded at Zack and they went to find the others to continue the shoot, but he had what he wanted for his ads, gorgeous photographs of Michaela now and later. He whispered to her as they went back to the crew.

"Don't say anything to the others. This is just between us. People get funny about things like that. Small minds."

"When will the center be open?" she asked him.

"In two weeks. We have some carpentry to put the finishing touches on, the rest of the art is arriving in a week, and we're done. I'm giving a little opening party," he said, speaking close to her. "I hope you can come."

The rest of the day slid by effortlessly and ended with

champagne and some informal portraits of the two of them. Then an Uber drove her back to West Hollywood, and she drifted up the stairs, feeling as though she had been in a magical place all day with a genius.

She tried to tell Billie about it when she got home, but it was all hard to put into words. She had forgotten all about the before and after pictures, which didn't seem important. It was just a little sleight of hand, and the way he explained it made perfect sense. She had no problem with it. She was the perfect partner for him. She had never had a strong attachment to the truth. The end had always justified the means since her earliest childhood and she still felt the same way about it.

Billie's first day at work had been more mundane, and she had enjoyed it. They had a wonderfully efficient pathology lab at Cedars-Sinai. She liked the people who worked there. The equipment was spectacular, thanks to enormous donations. She wasn't doing research as she had hoped to. She was performing tests, but it was good experience, and a pleasure to work for such a well-run institution. She needed the salary and it would look good on her resume for a first job. She was grateful that they had hired her.

Michaela went back to the house in Bel Air every day that week. Zack took gorgeous photographs of her. The house was coming together rapidly, and Alex was already living there. And being within the aura of Alex Addison was an extraordinary, almost out-of-body experience. She had never known anyone like him. Mickie felt as though he had cast a spell on her, but if it was true, she liked it. By the end of the week she had made twenty thousand dollars. She wasn't sure if she had sold her soul to the devil, or if he had. But Michaela had figured out that their ambitions were similar and dovetailed nicely, and Alex thought so too. Mickie was exactly the woman he wanted, with a brain and without a conscience, and with a gorgeous, flawless face.

Chapter 4

The shoot for Alex Addison's ad campaign went smoothly. He got all the looks, shots, and locations he wanted in it and Zack Campbell was fun to work with and brought out the best in Mickie. She was young and malleable and new enough in the business that she followed his directions to the letter, and Alex was always nearby, observing what was happening, and smiling at Mickie seductively. Her heart always beat a little faster when she knew Alex was watching her.

There were small crews of workmen floating around other parts of the house while they were there, and there were noticeable changes by the end of the week. Everything was looking more finished. In the medical part of the building there was his enormous, very lush-looking office, half a dozen exam rooms, a large central room with skylights and a glassed-in garden, offices for staff, a maze of supply rooms and storage spaces, and room for the office machines and lab equipment he was installing, all very efficient-looking. On the floor above, he had a fabulous apartment with an enormous bedroom, living room, study, guest room, a small pantry and kitchen setup, and a massive dressing room and marble bathroom for two. He had given Michaela a tour one afternoon when they finished shooting. The apartment had been finished before the office so he was already living there and settled in.

Mickie had noticed when she walked around the office with him that almost every door on the ground floor had a coded keypad in order to gain access. The office had a casual, modern, sensual, almost sexy feel, but there was nothing casual about his security systems. There were alarms and security cameras, and by the end of the week there was a security guard outside, wearing dark glasses and a black suit. The place had a mysterious feel to it, as though there was something very important and hush-hush going on inside.

"Will you need all that security?" Mickie asked him innocently, over a glass of wine in the sleek black granite kitchen when they finished shooting. There was a spectacular swimming pool too, with an infinity edge. The house had been very expensive, built by a well-known developer, and the installations Alex had made weren't cheap. It was obvious from his whole style that he could afford it, and he was sparing no expense to set up his Bel Air office. Before doing the built-ins he had taken a long lease on the house with an option to buy, and the owner was giving him a break on the rent, for the improvements he had made.

Alex Addison had the look of someone who had been wealthy all his life. He had an ease around luxury that only happened when you grew up with it. People with money gravitated toward him because they sensed immediately that he was one of them. He wasn't a newcomer or an outsider. Houses like his, and the world he moved in, were unfamiliar to Mickie, but he was the symbol of everything she wanted. He stunned her on the last day of the photo shoot by telling her to go through the rack of clothes and the accessories and keep anything she wanted. She was shocked when he said it. The stylist had pulled very expensive clothes from all the fanciest stores on Rodeo Drive. Alex told her the only thing she couldn't have was the borrowed jewelry from Van Cleef and Bulgari, which had to go back. But he was more than happy to buy the clothes for her, which didn't seem like such a big deal to him. Mickie filled three garment bags and two shopping bags with the pieces she liked. They were status symbols she had always dreamed of and never thought she'd own. There was a white Valentino jumpsuit that fit her like a second skin and looked fantastic on her. And a white Hermès Birkin bag that was her dream come true. Mickie knew all the most expensive luxury brands, but could never have afforded them in her wildest imagination. She asked Alex if he was sure she could have them, and he smiled at her and said of course, and walked her to the car waiting for her outside.

She could have sold the Birkin and paid her rent for a year, but she would rather cut off her arm than give it up. This was the chance of a lifetime. She had never met anyone like him. She thanked him again as she got into the car, and he put a hand on her arm and stopped her. She was afraid he was changing his mind about all the clothes she'd taken, and the Birkin, and he looked at her with eyes full of longing.

"Michaela, will you have dinner with me tonight? There's something I want to ask you." She didn't hesitate for an instant.

"Of course." She was flattered. He was twenty-three years older than she was, but incredibly sexy. He exuded youth and virility, elegance and charisma. He was wearing black jeans and a black T-shirt that showed his powerful, well-toned body, with his lab coat thrown over it, and black suede Hermès boots. He had a very European look, and he wore a version of that outfit as a uniform daily. He dressed all in black with his lab coat, like a medical version of Steve Jobs. His blond hair was perfectly cut. He looked like a film star interpretation of a doctor. He combined an air of authority with his good looks. It was an irresistible combination and they made a striking pair.

"Let's celebrate tonight. You made my advertising campaign this week. You are the face of Bellissima. Women are going to be begging to come and see me, hoping they'll become one-tenth as beautiful as you. Even I can't work that magic. Looks like yours come straight from heaven. I'll pick you up at seven-thirty. Give me your address." She gave him the address in West Hollywood, already mentally racing through her wardrobe, trying to think of the right thing to wear to "celebrate" with him. She wanted to dazzle him. He was everything she had always dreamed of, a gorgeous, rich, successful guy with a fabulous house and career. She couldn't guess what he wanted to ask her. She was ready to say yes before he even told her. "See you soon," he said as he closed the car door, and the driver pulled away a minute later. The agency had given her the chance of a lifetime, and she was going to make the most of it, while she had the chance.

*

Mickie tore through her closets as soon as she got home and decided to go all out for him. She picked a short, sexy Dior cocktail dress that showed off every inch of her flawless figure. She had the perfect high-heeled Manolo Blahnik sandals to go with it. She wore her hair loose down her back, and the dress had just enough cleavage to rivet his attention without being vulgar. She had an instinctive sense of just how far to go. She had just put the finishing touches on her outfit when Billie walked in from work at Cedars-Sinai. She looked at Mickie in surprise.

"Wow! You look incredible. Where are you going?" She figured maybe a movie premiere or some big deal event.

"Just out to dinner," Mickie said smugly.

"Lucky guy. Do you have a date or did they hire you to liven up an event?" Mickie got hired sometimes just to be somewhere and look gorgeous. It was easy money.

"I have a date," she said, smiling at her sister.

"I hope he's gorgeous and deserves you."

"It's Alex Addison."

"The doctor?" Billie wasn't really surprised. Who could resist a woman who looked like her sister? She had been practicing the art of seduction and looking gorgeous since she was thirteen, and she had reached the pinnacle of success, having dinner with the soon-to-be-famous new doctor in town. Mickie nodded in answer just as the intercom buzzed. She peeked out the window, and there was a silver Ferrari parked out front. She blew a kiss vaguely in Billie's direction, and flew past her out the door, hurrying down the steps to Alex waiting for her in the car.

When she got to the car, she opened the door on the passenger side and slid in as he beamed.

"You are a vision, my dear." He smiled happily, put the car into gear, and sped off, to an undisclosed destination of Alex's choosing. He had reserved for them at The Tower Bar, which she had heard of but never been to, and had dreamed of going there. She knew they had an indoor and outdoor space with a band next to the pool. She didn't care so much about dinner, but she loved the idea of being seen there, and with him. People stared at them when they arrived at the restaurant and were led to a table outdoors. They were the kind of couple that people loved to watch and guess who they were. They looked like Hollywood's biggest stars as they walked to their table, with Mickie's hips swaying gently, just enough to tease all the men who were watching, and especially Alex. She knew just how to achieve the desired effect.

They ordered martinis when they sat down, and Alex raised his glass in a toast when they arrived. He leaned close to her and said in a soft voice, "Thank you for making this week such a success, Mickie. You were fabulous. Yours is the face I want everyone to think of when they hear the word 'Bellissima.'" She was hoping to get a lot more work from it once his ads were out, maybe even a beauty campaign from a major brand. Her agency was hoping that too.

"Thank you for the opportunity, Alex," she said in a silky voice. She'd worn bright red lipstick and had sensual lips. They were sitting close together, side by side, his body close to hers.

"I have a proposition for you." He had planned to ask her at the end of the meal, but he couldn't wait. He'd been thinking about it all week. "I'd like you to be the ambassador for Bellissima, the person and face everyone thinks of when they hear the name. I'd like you to go to big events, openings, premieres. I'll pay for the clothes, of course. I want you to make a big splash in L.A., Michaela, and go to important social events with me. You're perfect for it. You could meet and greet people who come to Bellissima, men as well as women, and get to know my patients." It was a new concept in medicine, and he wasn't curing illnesses, he was dealing in beauty. It was an entirely different feeling. He told her the yearly salary he had in mind, and she nearly fell off her chair as she stared at him.

"Are you serious?" she asked him, and set her glass down.

"Very much so," he said in his deep sexy voice. He hoped he had quoted her enough. She looked so shocked he wasn't sure, as she put her long graceful arms around him and hugged him.

"I would love it! Yes, I accept!" He smiled broadly. He ordered caviar for them then, which she had never tasted. She knew she was supposed to love it, but she wasn't sure. But the rest of the meal was delicious. They had soufflés for dessert, and he ordered Cristal champagne, explaining to her it was the best one. He was going to teach her about all the finer things in life.

Mickie felt as though she had been waiting all her life for Alex to come along. She was excited at the prospect of going to major Hollywood events with him. He was intending to explore the celebrity side of L.A. and bring them in as clients. Once he had a few, he could hook them all. Alex Addison had big dreams too, and Michaela fit right into them. She was exactly what he needed as a welcoming committee to Bellissima, and the perfect woman to have on his arm. She would be the most beautiful woman in every room and he would get the credit for it. It was perfect.

"Oh, and one thing," he added as he signed the check for their dinner. Mickie glanced quickly and saw that it was three thousand dollars with tax and gratuity. It was by far the most expensive dinner she'd ever eaten, and maybe ever would. "I thought of it the other day. I'd like you to tell our patients and the people you meet in your new role that you're thirty-three years old. Kind of our little private joke. It'll unsettle them if they know how young you are. I think thirty-three is much more reassuring, and you can attribute your youthful beauty to our treatments." It was no different than the before and after photos, and it didn't bother her at all.

"For what you're paying me to be your ambassador, Alex, I'll tell them I'm a hundred if you like. It makes me feel suddenly very grown-up to be thirty-three. I like it. People will respect me more." She looked happy.

"They'll respect you because you'll be with me," he said, and they left the restaurant together. He put his arm around her as they walked to the valet and asked for the Ferrari. He had rented it for the evening to impress her and it had. He usually drove an SUV, which wasn't the sexy image he wanted to portray to her. Whatever the reason, money, prestige, sex appeal, she had accepted his offer to be his ambassador. He was creating a world and an ambiance around it that no one would be able to resist. And Michaela was now part of that package. It was just a little touch of marketing and good business. And given the positive nature of his practice, he saw no harm in blending business and medicine. He wasn't hurting anyone. He was giving them greater beauty and improving their confidence and their lives. It was all for the greater good. He saw himself as the benefactor of all the women he would be treating. It was a holy mission for him, and he had found the perfect woman to represent him, the ideal partner for his new venture. The valet brought the car around, and Alex took Mickie in his arms and kissed her. The passion that had been bubbling just below the surface all week suddenly surged through them as he pressed against her and she could feel him come alive as they kissed. They finally moved apart, breathless, and got into the car.

"Would you like to come over for a drink?" he asked her in a voice hoarse with passion, as he leaned over and kissed her again, and she nodded. There was no hesitation. She was nineteen years old, but she was no innocent, even if she came from a much simpler background than he did. He had finally met his match, and she had met hers. She had been waiting for him all her life, and now that she had found him, nothing was going to stop her from hanging on, and following him to wherever he wanted her to go.

He gunned the car and drove back to Bel Air as quickly as he dared, before she could change her mind. They left the car in his driveway and walked past the security guard on duty, who nodded respectfully at them both.

Alex unlocked the front door and kissed her as soon as

they closed the door. She left her handbag and shoes downstairs, and they raced up the stairs to his apartment, and were already half undressed when they got to his bedroom, with an enormous king-size bed. She stood for a moment as he peeled the dress away from her exquisite body, and she undid his trousers as he dropped his shirt and the rest of his clothes on the floor and they fell into his bed. She was an experienced woman who knew exactly how to please him, far beyond what her tender age would have suggested. Mickie had made a point of learning what men wanted and how to drive them mad, starving for what they wanted from her. It was a dance of experts in his bed, of lust and desire, taunting, teasing, tormenting, begging. They were equal partners and came together in a searing white hot fire and then lay completely spent. Mickie had never met anyone like him before among the men she slept with, and Alex owned her from that moment. He had never met a woman who could drive him into a frenzy of desire the way she could. She was made up in equal parts of torture and pleasure, and he wasn't sure which he liked most. The whole package was one he had always longed to find, and now he had. They were trapped somewhere between heaven and hell. She was part devil and part angel, and he was smiling as he made love to her again, several times before the night was over. Their coupling was pure desire and had nothing to do with love, and neither of them had to pretend otherwise. It was the best night of their lives and a promising beginning to their new adventure.

Billie didn't wait up for Mickie to come home. She wanted to do some reading in one of her old textbooks. She read three chapters and made some notes of things that might apply to the testing she was doing. She went to bed early, figuring that Mickie might come in late. She had no desire to babysit her little sister. They were two grown women sharing an apartment, with different tastes and jobs and lifestyles. She wasn't there to pass judgment on her sister. And she doubted that Mickie's interest in dining with the doctor was romantic. She had done a job for him that week and he'd paid her well, and Billie suspected she probably accepted the invitation more for the free meal than anything else. He was twice her age, and Billie was still skeptical about the "beauty center" for special techniques and nonsurgical treatments. It sounded a little shady to her, or certainly more commercial than medical. The mention Mickie had made of before and after pictures sounded flat-out dishonest, if Mickie had understood the doctor correctly. Hopefully she was confused about how he intended to use them. What Mickie had said couldn't have been right.

When Billie stuck her head in the open door of Mickie's room on Saturday morning, she realized that her sister hadn't come home that night, which surprised her. She thought Mickie must have met up with friends after dinner with the doctor. She didn't report to Billie and wouldn't have called to tell her if she wasn't coming home. Billie's standing in in a parental role had ended four years before, and Mickie owed her no explanations. It was a beautiful day, and Billie could hear a few people chatting around the pool. She decided to go downstairs and check it out. She had an old faded one-piece bathing suit left over from her high school days on the swim team. She didn't own a whole drawer full of bikinis the way Mickie did for trade shows, and didn't need them. She put her bathing suit on, with cut-off shorts and one of her bottomless supply of MIT T-shirts, slipped on a pair of sandals, finished her coffee, and went downstairs to join the other tenants at the pool. By the time she got there, the two couples she'd noticed with a child had left, there were two women lying on deck chairs at one end of the pool, and a man lying face down on the other side, sleeping in the sun with a copy of the *Los Angeles Times* lying next to him, and a thick book about the death of communism. She sat down in a chair halfway between him and the women, and pulled out the biology book she wanted to reread over the weekend.

Half an hour later the two women left, and the man at the far end had turned over on his back and was reading the book on communism. He didn't acknowledge Billie's presence, and she only glanced at him once, wondering who would read such a boring book. He had an athletic body and long legs, and was wearing sunglasses, and she liked the fact that she could read there peacefully and no one would talk to her. The pool was apparently not used as a meeting place or dating rendezvous in the building. There weren't groups of tenants getting drunk together, or a flock of guys with a cooler of beer. The building was quiet and the tenants discreet, which suited her perfectly. She had finished two more chapters and put the book down, as the other tenant walked past her with his newspaper and book, glanced at her book on the chair next to her, and smiled. He looked at Billie, and spoke to her in a casual friendly way. He was wearing swim trunks and a Columbia T-shirt, and his hair, as dark as hers, looked as though he hadn't bothered to brush it.

"I think we both win the prize for most boring books read at a swimming pool on any given day. Sorry, I couldn't help but notice. Biology? Where do you go to school?" he asked her. She pointed to her faded T-shirt, one of her oldest.

"Except I graduated. I'm not sure communism is much more interesting."

"I agree with you. I've been trying to finish it for two months, and every time I pick it up, I fall asleep. Did you really go to MIT?" She nodded. "That's a pretty unusual school for a woman, except if you want to be a physics professor or an engineer. I'm sorry if that sounds sexist. I don't mean it to be."

"I was a biology major." She pointed to his shirt. "Did you go to Columbia?" She was just being neighborly, although she noticed that he was nice-looking, despite the unruly hair. He looked like he was in his mid-thirties, ten years older than she was.

"School of Journalism," he answered her question. "I went to UCLA undergrad. I liked it here so I came back." He lingered in order to talk to her. There was something about the way she looked that he liked. She was unfussy and looked normal and natural. She didn't have a lot of airs and graces, and didn't have the artificial look of a lot of the women he met in L.A., mostly ambitious young actresses and models. And his female colleagues at work were very competitive and intense. He had no desire to compete with them, which they would have liked. It was a new breed of women these days, anxious to prove that they were superior to men in every way and didn't need them. Several of the women he knew at work had gone to sperm banks to have babies, saying they didn't need a man to start a family. His mother was an attorney in New York, but she was warm and gentle and feminine. She specialized in intellectual property and literary law. "Where are you from?" he asked her. No one he knew was from California. They all came from somewhere else originally.

"I'm from Iowa," she said, feeling shy for an instant.

"I'm from New York," he said. He would have liked to sit down next to her but didn't want to intrude. "No one is ever from California. It fascinates me. Does no one grow up here?"

"Probably not." She smiled at him.

"Have you been here long?" he asked her.

"Two weeks." He smiled again at her answer.

"See what I mean?" he said. "Are you from Des Moines? I went there once for work."

"I grew up on a dairy farm in Collins, Iowa," she said sheepishly. "With a population of five hundred."

"Can you milk a cow?" he asked, amused at the image, and she laughed. He couldn't imagine it.

"Definitely."

"Now that begs for further conversation. A girl from Iowa who grew up on a dairy farm and went to MIT. Are you in med school?"

"Nope, I work at Cedars-Sinai. I'm hoping to get a job in a research lab with a pharmaceutical company, but I got here two weeks ago and needed a job, so I work at the pathology lab there."

"I work at the *L.A. Times,* in crime. I want to work in politics, but so does everyone else, so I'm stuck with crime for now. I was a political science major at UCLA."

"That's kind of how I feel about working in the lab at Cedars, waiting for a better opportunity, but I'm enjoying it more than I thought I would."

"I think half the people working here are in a temporary job, waiting for something else, or they're actors or musicians out of work. It's very L.A." His smile grew into a grin. "Would you like to discuss it over dinner sometime? And I'm sorry, I'm Jason Bell." He held out a hand and they shook hands.

"Billie Banks."

"Interesting name too." He looked intrigued. He liked her, she seemed normal and sane and smart. And pretty.

"Wilhelmina."

"Even better. Is it too blunt to ask you for your number, or should I just stick a note under your door to invite you to dinner?" She laughed, and told him her number and he put it in his phone. "I'll send you a text. There's a pretty good Mexican restaurant down the street if you like spicy food."

"That sounds great." He went back to his apartment a

few minutes later, and she thought about him. She liked him too. He seemed nice and straightforward, with an interesting job, more so than hers. He reminded her a little of her friend Tom Carter, not like some of the people they went to school with, mean bitchy girls, and guys who just wanted to drink beer and get laid, with no ambition. She and Tom had never fit in with most of their peers. A political science major who was a crime reporter sounded like fun to her. He was certainly worth having one dinner with to check it out. She had liked talking to him.

Mickie came home in her black cocktail dress a few hours later, packed a small bag for the weekend, and left again. Alex was waiting for her in the Ferrari while she rushed into the apartment to pack. She told Billie she didn't know when she'd be back. She said Alex was the most amazing man she'd ever met. There were signs of the old Mickie of their youth, sex-driven and always having some wild impulsive fling, now with her new boss, which didn't seem like a good idea to Billie. But she knew better than to warn her, or try to reason with her. She just waved when Mickie ran out the door, after flying around the apartment for ten minutes gathering what she wanted. She hoped that Mickie knew what she was doing and wouldn't regret it, but there was no stopping her when she had a new man in her sights.

In the past she had turned vicious whenever Billie tried to reason with her.

Billie finished reading her biology book over the weekend. She got a text from Jason on Sunday, inviting her to dinner at the Mexican restaurant on Monday night, and she accepted. Mickie hadn't come home yet, and Billie had no idea when she would, and didn't worry about her. Mickie could take care of herself. She always had. Billie knew better than to try to stop her.

Chapter 5

Alex Addison spent the weekend wining and dining Mickie, when they weren't having unbridled sex all over his apartment. They had dinner on Saturday night at the Polo Lounge at the Beverly Hills Hotel, with several famous people close enough to touch at nearby tables. Mickie was in the big leagues now and she wasn't going to do anything to blow it. She was an ambitious girl with a hunger for a much better life and willing to do whatever she needed to do to get there, and to stay now that she'd arrived. A handsome, rich, successful doctor was a lucky break, and he was crazy about her and couldn't get enough of her. She took full advantage of it.

Mickie had improved on her natural skills after she got to L.A., and she had learned some tricks in bed that drove him insane. She was willing to do and try almost anything, far beyond what most women would do, and he loved the wild side of her. They were madly in lust, and he didn't have to claim emotions for her he didn't feel. She didn't care about that. He wanted to possess her body in every way he could, and she surprised him frequently in bed, which he wouldn't have believed possible. She was totally at ease with her own body and his, and bolder than any woman he'd ever met, and he was twice her age. She didn't mind that either. He had never met a woman as hungry for sex as he was.

They spent Sunday on a sexual marathon, and on Sunday night, he put five thousand dollars in cash on the kitchen table, where they had just made love again. For a minute she thought he was paying her, which made her uncomfortable. She wasn't his hooker and had never taken money for sex. She gave it away to whomever, how and when she wanted to. He hadn't bought her, even though she worked for him now. He felt like he had won the lottery when he met her. It was the most exciting weekend of his life. He couldn't get enough of her.

"What's that for?" she asked, and didn't touch the bills lying on the table next to her. Her voice was cold when she asked. She could go from hot to cold in seconds, and back again.

"I've been invited to a party given by the head of a

streaming service," Alex explained. "His wife is my best patient. I want you to come with me. Buy yourself something fabulous to wear. If that's not enough, call me, and I'll have my assistant take care of it," he said, and she felt relief wash over her. He wasn't treating her like a hooker after all. To reward him, she inflicted unexpected pain on him and he loved it. She loved causing him pain, it excited them both. "Thank you," she said for the money for the dress. They spent another night of reciprocal torment and ecstasy, and he looked relaxed and happy on Monday morning, and told her she'd better leave before his medical staff started arriving. He said they were filling the supply closets that day with his secret formulas.

"Is that why you have code locks on all the doors in the office?" She had noticed it when he walked her through.

"I don't want anyone stealing the formulas it took me years to develop," he said seriously. "They're worth a fortune. It's why I have security at the door. And there will be more once we're open." She was impressed by what he said. She had hit the jackpot, in every way. The weekend had proved it to both of them. He was as convinced as she was, and he liked that she could look and behave like a lady in public and a tornado in bed. He had never before encountered that combination in one woman. She was a rare find.

"Where did you go to college?" he asked her while he

made her breakfast, and she lay stretched out on the counter naked. He had to control himself not to lunge at her again, but they didn't have time. He was already dressed for work in a black shirt and black jeans, with black alligator cowboy boots. He didn't have his doctor's coat on yet.

"Stanford," Mickie answered, taunting him with her legs wide apart. There was a thin film of perspiration on his forehead, while he put scrambled eggs on a plate for her. Because she'd been hired as a model, he'd never seen an application that referred to her education. "I took this year off, to do some modeling. I'm going back in January," she said casually, unzipping his jeans with agonizing slowness.

"That's a great school," he said in a strangled voice, barely able to breathe, as she freed him from his jeans, and they both forgot the eggs. "You're a very smart girl. Lucky for me you took the year off." She gave him what he wanted then. They knocked over two chairs, and the plate broke on the floor and spilled the eggs neither of them cared about. It was over in minutes, and he stood smiling at her, as she lay on the kitchen counter. All he could think of was how glad he was that he had hired her. He could have an unlimited diet of Mickie whenever he wanted, any way he desired. She would be right there with him all the time every day.

She hopped off the table then and ran upstairs to dress, while he cleaned up the eggs and smoothed down his hair.

She was back in five minutes, looking prim in jeans, a white blouse, and ballet slippers, with her hair in a knot at her neck. She looked beautiful and normal, and not like the wild woman he had discovered on the weekend. She hid the truth remarkably well.

"Do you want to come by for lunch?" he asked her, and she smiled coolly.

"I have a go-see." She didn't, but she didn't want to be too available.

"Tonight?" He felt like the supplicant, and would have hated her for it, except he wanted her so badly. He couldn't get enough of her. He was already starving for her. And they were going to the party he'd invited her to that night.

She called an Uber and kissed him primly. The five thousand dollars he had given her the night before was in her purse.

"Besides, I have to shop for the dress you want me to get. What time is the party?"

"Eight o'clock. I'll pick you up at seven-thirty, unless you want to dress here. But we might never get out the door. And tonight is important. We have to go." It was going to be her debut as his ambassadress and his woman, so she was eager to go too. She was curious to discover the world he moved in, the people he knew.

"I'll be camera-ready when you come," she assured him. "We can always have a little extra fun at the party," she said playfully and he looked serious.

"Tonight's important, Michaela. We can't get crazy there. They're decent people . . . not like us," he added. Michaela was a bad girl to the core and he loved it.

"Of course not," she said, looking demure. She kissed him as the Uber arrived, and she was out the door with her bag and his money and a day of shopping ahead of her. She would be flawless at the party. She knew just how to do it. She waved as the Uber drove away and he stood staring after it, wondering what had hit him. His medical staff arrived ten minutes later, and they started unpacking the boxes of his medical supplies, and placing them where he directed them to. Each time the doors locked behind them, and they had to use the code again. He intended to change the code every day, more often if he had to. No one was going to steal his secrets, or the woman he had found, who in one short stunning week he had already discovered he couldn't live without. Michaela Banks was the most unusual, extraordinary, exciting woman he had ever met. He could hardly wait for the party tonight, but he had work to do in the meantime. And his secret formulas to lock up to protect them.

*

When Mickie left Alex's house, she went home to drop off her things. Alex didn't expect her to be at his office for regular office hours, just to drop in, meet patients at times, and go to parties with him. It didn't even feel like a job. She called the agency to check in and see if they had anything for her. They had her on hold for two go-sees later in the week, but didn't have a confirmation yet. After that, she took off to Rodeo Drive to spend Alex's five thousand dollars, to buy a dress for that night. She started at one end of the street and worked her way down. She wandered around Ralph Lauren, saw a peach-colored sundress she liked, but decided to come back if she had money left after the "something fabulous" he had told her to buy. She walked into Chanel, and looked no different than the other girls her age shopping there. She was wearing white jeans, a pink sweater, ballet flats she had bought at her secondhand store, and the white Birkin bag Alex had given her from the shoot. It was an incredibly generous gift, as was the five thousand dollars she had in it, to shop with that day.

She saw a dozen things she wanted to buy, but none of them was dressy enough for that night. She went to Gucci and didn't see anything she liked, then Valentino. She was beginning to panic when she stopped in at Prada, and the dress on the mannequin looked like what Alex had in mind.

It was a short silver knit dress, with sleeves made of black and silver feathers. They showed it with black stockings and silver shoes, and a big rhinestone necklace. It was a knockout, and Mickie asked to see it in her size. She was afraid it would cost more than Alex had given her, but he had told her to call his office if she needed more. She was trying to stay within the budget so he didn't think she was greedy. They took the dress off the mannequin for her to try. The sleeves floated with the feathers. They left it with her in the dressing room, and went to get the shoes in her size. And they had a small silver clutch with rhinestones that matched. She tried on the whole outfit the mannequin had been wearing and it looked incredible on her. The dress was very short but she had the legs to get away with it, long and slim like her father's, and the dress clung to her just enough in the right places to be sexy but not obscene. It looked like something she would wear in a modeling shoot but could never own. Mickie glanced at the price tag, and it was less than anything she'd seen at Chanel and seemed to fit Alex's description of fabulous, and the salesgirl smiled when she came back with the shoes.

"That dress hasn't looked like that on anyone who's tried it. It was made for you." The black feather arms floated to her wrists like swan wings, and the silver knit dress showed every inch of her figure, and the shoes fit perfectly. The rhinestone necklace and clutch made the outfit, along with sheer black stockings with tiny rhinestones scattered on them like stars. Mickie looked like the cover of *Vogue* and felt like a million dollars, and she had seventy dollars left in her Birkin when she carried her package out of the store. She had the perfect outfit. It was just what he had asked for. Something fabulous. She went back to the apartment, laid it all out on her bed, and went to lie on a deck chair at the pool. She felt as though she had won the lottery and couldn't wait until Alex saw her outfit that night. She hoped he liked the look for the party they were going to. He said it was an important event and an opportunity to meet new patients. His most important patient had organized it for him. He said that social appearances were an important part of meeting new patients, and Mickie was part of his image now. The subliminal message was that if she was that beautiful and looked that young, he must have had something to do with it, particularly if she said she was thirty-three, not nineteen. Mickie never minded lying for a good cause. Sometimes she lied just for the hell of it or because it was fun.

She stayed at the pool till six and went back to the apartment to get ready. She was in the shower when Billie came home from work. It had been an interesting day at work. She had been assigned to do breast biopsies. The hospital had an important breast health clinic. She helped herself to a snack in the kitchen, and stuck her head into Mickie's room to say hello and saw the silver dress hanging on the door of one of Mickie's closets. She had hogged them all, but Billie didn't care, she hardly had any clothes.

"Wow! What's that?" Billie looked at the silver dress and touched the sleeves, as Mickie walked into the room. The feathers floated and were light as air. Billie had plans herself that night and had stopped in Mickie's room when she came out of the shower, and was wrapped in a towel.

"I just got it today," Mickie said proudly.

"At your secondhand place?"

Mickie nodded. "Umm . . . yeah . . . It was dirt cheap."

"It must look incredible on you." She went to get dressed herself then, while Mickie got ready for her big evening.

She did her hair in a sleek bun, did her makeup, and put the whole outfit back together with the necklace, and Billie gasped when she saw the full effect. It was dazzling, and the rhinestones on the necklace and stockings flashed like iridescent stars.

"You look amazing," she said to her little sister in a tone of awe, not envy. When she saw Mickie dressed, it reminded Billie of a dress Mickie had worn one year as prom queen with a rhinestone bustier. She had sparkled like the disco ball at the party when she was crowned. She had a knack for pulling together stunning outfits.

Mickie was ready when Alex arrived on the dot of seven-thirty and called her from the car. She asked him if he wanted to come up and meet her sister and Alex responded, "Another time. I don't want to be late. I want a chance to speak to the relevant guests as they arrive." He had no interest in Mickie's family, only in her.

"Have a fun evening," Billie said as Mickie sailed past her and hurried down the stairs in the silver high heels, and down the walk to where Alex was waiting. He still had the Ferrari for the rest of the week. He was wearing a black Tom Ford tuxedo with a black shirt. He was all in black as usual, but on him it didn't look ominous, it looked elegant and dramatic, as she did. His eyes grew wide when he saw Mickie. He hadn't been prepared for the impact she would make but he loved it.

"Oh my God, Michaela, I said 'fabulous,' not 'give me cardiac arrest when I see you.'"

"Is it too flashy?" She looked panicked.

"No, you look like a star fallen straight from heaven, it's perfect."

"I have seventy dollars left for you," she said proudly, relieved that he liked it. "I got the whole outfit at Prada."

"It's a knockout. You're the best advertisement I could have." Every woman in the room would envy her look, her dress, her perfect body, her exquisite face. He was pleased on the way to the party, and heads turned when they got there, and everyone stared at her as Alex made his way to their hostess, with Mickie's hand tucked firmly into his arm. Every woman there was wearing a gorgeous designer dress, but Mickie's was the shortest, brightest, and sexiest, and she was by far the youngest and most beautiful woman there.

Their hostess, Marilyn Hodges, kissed him on the cheek and Mickie noticed that she was nice-looking and had lovely skin and a smooth face. She was in her late fifties and no longer had a face or figure like Mickie's, or never had. She was wearing a pink brocade cocktail dress with a matching jacket, which was a little tight on her. Alex had met her at a spa in Miami. Mickie was dazzled by the clothes and the jewels she was seeing around her. She took a glass of champagne from a tray, as the hostess took Alex around and introduced him to her friends, whispering to each of them that he was the magician she had told them about. Their faces lit up at the introduction, and Alex was attentive and charming to each of them.

"When are you opening your new center, Doctor?" one of the guests asked him.

"We're putting the finishing touches on now, and we'll be fully open next week, but I can sneak you in this week, if you like," he whispered back, and the woman beamed.

He made each woman feel special, and the hostess most of all. The hostess whispered in his ear.

"Tomorrow?" she asked, hopeful, and he nodded with a smile and gave her a hug.

"I have your special formula waiting for you. I put it in the fridge for you myself today. No name on it, of course, just your number." He was planning to do everything with the utmost secrecy. He wanted all his patients to feel special, and he made it clear that they were to him.

Alex circulated in the crowd all evening, talking to beautiful women, and their hostess explained how remarkable he was and called him a genius.

When appropriate, he would have Mickie join them, or if not, at a subtle sign from him, she would drift away, and one of the men at the party would join her within minutes. She was the hit of the evening in her dress, and Alex in his tuxedo with the black shirt, with unlimited charm, as he introduced himself. And their hostess did the rest. Those who wanted it would all have his number by the next day. Alex knew how to work a crowd without ever being obvious about it. He was very efficient, and Mickie was impressed after watching him in action.

"What kind of treatments do you give them?" she asked as they moved from one group to another. He was like a magnet to women over thirty-five once they knew who he was. And Marilyn talked about him a lot to her friends. He was alternately boyish, charming, or seductive with them, depending on the subtle cues he got.

"The usual procedures," Alex answered vaguely. "Botox for some, some collagen, laser treatments, fillers, we've been doing a lot of collagen thread lifts, Thermage, meso-therapy, and I have some magic potions that work miracles," he said mysteriously.

"Should I get any of that?" Mickie looked intrigued. She'd never considered it before.

"At your age?" he laughed. "Don't be ridiculous. We'll talk about it in five years. Until then, you can have a lollipop and a Barbie Band-Aid if you scrape your knee," he said, and she laughed. It was magical being with him. And after the party, the moment they walked into his house, before he even switched on the lights, her shimmering silvery dress with the black and silver plumage lay on the white marble floor. They only made it as far as the sleek white Italian couch in his waiting area, with the subtly lit pool beyond. Both of them were naked within an instant and her whole body was electrified by his touch. They began making love on the couch, and when she straddled him he carried her outside to the pool. She felt as light in his arms as the feathers on the dress she had worn, he slipped naked into the pool with her, and they continued making love in the warm water. They were hidden from view, and she teased and tormented him in all the ways she had discovered were what he liked best. He came with a shuddering surge and a shout of exquisite agony. She pulled away afterward and swam away from him, and he followed her to the deep end of the pool, where she perched on a wide step and he took her again. He fought her for control, and she bewitched him once more. She was a strong swimmer, and their sensual dance continued as he pulled her deeper underwater, and held her there in his powerful arms. He only released her when she thought her lungs would burst, and she came while gasping for air when she reached the surface, and she took vengeance on him until he begged for mercy. It was Mickie who won in the end. They were like two beautiful sea creatures in a primal dance that went on long into the night until at last they were spent, and fell asleep on a lounge chair, naked and exquisite in the moonlight.

Billie's night out was very different from her sister's. As different as they were.

Jason Bell had an apartment a floor above Billie and Mickie's. He came by to pick her up at eight, after Mickie had left for her Cinderella evening with Alex. Jason drove Billie to the restaurant in his battered Jeep, with the top down, not in a Ferrari. He was wearing a crisp white shirt, jeans, and loafers, and she was wearing a flowered blouse, white jeans, and sandals, with her dark hair loose down her back. She looked young and pretty and fresh.

The restaurant was crowded and fun. There was an outdoor terrace, where they got a table, and a terrific mariachi band played for the first hour. Billie loved the music, they drank margaritas, and the food was delicious. There was a festive atmosphere, and when the band left, Billie and Jason chatted over dinner. He talked about growing up in New York. His mother was an intellectual property attorney and represented several famous writers, and his father was the head of a well-known, respected publishing house. Jason had gone to private schools in New York, and was faintly embarrassed to admit that he had had a comfortable, privileged life with loving parents. He had gone to college on the West Coast to get away from them and have a normal life "without someone ironing my jeans and doing my laundry and solving all my problems for me. After I graduated from UCLA, I went back to New York for grad school, at the Columbia School of Journalism, but I lived in a rat's nest apartment with two other guys to pay penance for going to my parents' place in Connecticut on the weekends. I really like my parents. They're good people, with good values. I have a terrific sister, Emily, who's two years older than I am. She's thirty-five, a novelist, and lives in Vermont with a guy I like a lot. He's a country doctor, a GP. My sister has had two novels published so far, not big bestsellers yet, but she's good. She went to Middlebury and liked it so much she stayed in Vermont, and that's how she met Thad, Thaddeus MacAdams. His family has been in Vermont for generations. She loves the country life. I'm a city boy. I love New York, but I like living out here too. I moved here three years ago when I turned thirty, and I was momentarily fed up with New York. I have a love-hate relationship with the city," he said, and she laughed. "So what was Iowa like?" he asked her and she thought about it for a minute, thinking about how to describe it.

"I never fit in. Weirdly, neither did my sister. She was too glamorous and wanted the fast life, so she dropped out of high school, got her GED, left, and came out here. But she was the coolest girl at school and the prom queen every year at home in Iowa. And I was the nerdy, geeky one whom all the cool girls made fun of. My best friend all through school was a guy. He's in the Middle East now, doing counterterrorist missions in the army. I never see him anymore since he's been undercover, but we were best friends till he graduated from West Point, and shipped out when he got into military intelligence.

"My mother was the glue that held our family together," she said wistfully. "She never went past high school, got married as soon as she graduated, and had me. She didn't go to college, but she read everything she could lay her hands on. My father doesn't believe in education, for anyone, men or women, he thinks it's all nonsense. He's an old-fashioned farmer, owns a small dairy. My mother died when I was seventeen and my sister was fourteen, and it all fell apart after that. I was a science nut and got into MIT on a full scholarship. I graduated in May and now here I am. I wanted to stay in Boston. I loved it, but I couldn't find a job, so I came out here to share an apartment with my sister. She's modeling, and she just took a job with some weird doctor. He's a Harvard-trained plastic surgeon who doesn't believe in surgery, so he does noninvasive treatments with some sort of miracle drugs and makes people look young again. I can't tell if he's a charlatan or not. I'm pretty skeptical about that kind of thing. But he hired my sister to be the symbol of youthful beauty for his medical beauty center. That kind of thing seems a little too narcissistic for me," she said.

"Are you and your sister very close?" he asked her, touched by her story and how openly she told it, without dressing it up or hiding anything or making it better than it was.

"No," she answered him bluntly about Mickie. "I hated her growing up. She did all the worst stuff, I mean really awful stuff, and blamed me. My father always believed her, so did our teachers and other parents. The only one who didn't believe her was my mother. Mickie was a little witch as a kid, and I was always punished for her crimes. I swore I'd never trust her again, and now here I am, living with her. But I have to admit, she's been really nice, and I'm actually enjoying her. I just don't trust her completely. But it looks like she's grown up while I was in college. She's young, she's only nineteen, but she's always been very advanced for her age. She was having sex while I was milking the cows and playing with dolls, and she's three years younger!" she said, and he laughed at her honesty.

"I think a lot of siblings fight when they're kids, and are best friends later. My sister and I had a few nasty rows, mostly because she was older and lorded it over me. She was taller until I was fifteen, and then I shot up. Before that, she used to beat me up. But we're good friends now. I love her books, and I hope she really makes it big one of these days."

"I can't say I had a normal childhood," Billie said. "I'm not even sure what that is. You'd think life on a farm in Iowa would be as ordinary as it gets. But it isn't. Maybe some people there are normal. The ones I knew married too young, were unhappy, got trapped there, cheat on their spouses, and drink too much." She thought of her father. "I don't think they're happy. I couldn't wait to get out, and I wanted an education. My mother was determined to see that I got one. In the end, my high school counselor got me into MIT, which was my ticket to freedom. I couldn't go back now, except for a visit. I go home for Christmas every year, but that's it."

"Are you happy?" Jason asked her gently.

She thought about it before she answered. "Yes, I think I am. L.A. is kind of fun. I like my job. I want a better job when I can get one. But I like going to work every day. I loved MIT and everything I learned there. I got the education I wanted, and one day I'll get the job, and I'm not trapped on a farm in Iowa. I can go wherever I want. I'm free. All those mean girls I went to school with, who were such bitches to me because I was smart and I wasn't cool, are miserable now. So yes, I am happy. Are you?"

"I'm kind of like you," he said. "Though in my case I'm close to my family so I always have them to fall back on, which is lucky for me. I love New York, but I love L.A. too. I like my job but I don't love it. I'm eleven years older than you are so I feel more pressure about the job. I want to cover politics, not homicides, but I don't hate going to work every day, and I figure I'll get to where I want eventually.

I worry about getting complacent and too comfortable and not pushing myself hard enough. I try to watch out for that.

"I've had a couple of nice relationships with women I liked and didn't want to marry, and we're still friends. I've never been madly in love or felt compelled to get married, so maybe I have a Peter Pan complex. My parents think men shouldn't marry till they're thirty-five, so I have this illusion that I have time, but most of the people I went to school with have kids by now. I definitely don't feel ready for that. I'm kind of coasting along, feeling good. Maybe I'm not ambitious enough, but California does that to you. You get comfortable here and don't push yourself. But New York is so driven, it's too much. I have a nice time in my life. It's all I need for right now," he said, and he smiled. He was in fact very normal, and she liked that about him. He didn't have any deep-seated damage, he was just a nice, smart guy who liked his family and had a good job. "I have a lot to be grateful for," he said, and she agreed, but she did too. She had a roof over her head, she had found a decent job, and she was living with her sister and it seemed to be working out. She hadn't run out of money, although she had come close, and she was going to be able to pay her share of the rent with the job at Cedars-Sinai. All her needs were being met. And now she had met a guy she liked. He seemed respectable, he was fun, smart, and had an interesting job. She thought being a crime reporter sounded fascinating, even if he liked politics better. He was well educated, and his family sounded like a dream come true to her, compared to growing up with a father who had ignored her and overlooked her for all her life, and the sister from hell, although admittedly, Mickie seemed to have improved markedly since she grew up and left home. She wasn't even a bad roommate. Billie wondered what her sudden affair with her new boss would turn into. It had taken off at jet speed, which was always Mickie's style, but he sounded like a big-deal fancy guy to Billie. She didn't know why but she had a strange feeling about him. He sounded so flashy and so showy from everything Mickie said that she wondered if he was for real. But Mickie always seized the opportunities that came and made the best of them. And Alex Addison sounded like the biggest opportunity she'd ever had. Billie thought he was too old for her too, but Mickie didn't care. He had a gorgeous house, an expensive car, he was incredibly handsome, and he was generous with her. It was all she wanted for now.

The evening with Jason ended on a gentle note. They sat in the lounge chairs at the pool for a while, looking at the sky over L.A. He went and got a bottle of wine from his apartment after a while and poured them each a glass. She'd had two margaritas at dinner, but the meal they'd eaten had neutralized them. She didn't feel drunk, just lazy and relaxed. She felt slightly tipsy with the wine, but she enjoyed his company. Jason seemed very grown-up, sane and well balanced. She liked that he had such a stable background and wasn't getting over some horrendous trauma in his youth. He was polite and kind, intelligent, and attentive to her. After half an hour he walked her back to her apartment. They both had work the next day.

"I really had a nice time," he told her before he left. She didn't invite him in. There was nowhere comfortable to sit, between the sagging couch and an equally ugly chair. Mickie had bought the barest essentials when she moved in.

"So did I." Billie smiled at him, feeling shy for a minute. She didn't know if he was going to try to kiss her, and it seemed like too soon. She was relieved when he didn't. She had only met him two days before. She was hoping he'd ask her out again. And he was smiling when he went upstairs to his apartment, thinking of her.

Billie wasn't surprised when Mickie didn't come home that night. She would have been stunned if she had, and disappointed for her. In the outfit she was wearing, her little sister was out to conquer the world, with an important new man at the end of her line. Billie knew that Mickie would stop at nothing until he was addicted to her, and she knew just how to do it. It was only a matter of time before she caught him and had him hooked. Knowing her sister, the only question that remained in Billie's mind was when.

Chapter 6

Alex was in a black T-shirt and jeans with his white coat, waiting for Marilyn Hodges, their hostess of the night before, when she arrived at nine the next morning. His office wasn't open yet, but he had seen her text on his phone when he and Mickie had finally gone to his bedroom at four A.M. and he had set his alarm for eight. He took his practice and his patients seriously.

Marilyn was a slightly overweight, moderately attractive blonde woman. She was turning sixty and spent a fortune on her appearance and her clothes. She was the wife of one of the most successful men in Hollywood, the head of an important streaming platform. Their marriage had been shaky for years, and she was well aware of the scores of other, younger women in her husband's life. He was extremely generous with her as a result. He had no desire for an astronomically expensive divorce, and let her spend whatever she wanted to keep her happy. She arrived as though meeting her drug dealer, almost shaking with anticipation. Alex had met her two years before at the opening of an ultra-luxurious spa in Miami, and she had given him the idea of moving his practice to L.A. His nonsurgical elite practice in Palm Beach had been a discreet secret for several years, and had grown exponentially by word of mouth. He had perfected his new techniques there. It began with a select few clients and had expanded. His most devoted patients had enlisted their husbands as the first investors in the center he had just opened in Bel Air. Marilyn looked around the new center for the first time. Her husband, Roger, had paid for a good part of it. Alex was treating her for free to thank her for all the patients she had sent him, literally almost all her friends in L.A. He had recently tried some of his newest procedures on her with excellent results. She said he had magic hands. She was willing to try anything he suggested. She had total faith in him and loved the result of the fillers he used and gave her with shots.

He led her into one of the beautiful treatment rooms after she had looked around. She was proud of the contribution her husband had made to help him set it up. Alex always did fillers on her lips and face. She never asked him what he used, she didn't care, she loved the end result. He was like a sculptor making each patient more beautiful than she'd been before. She'd already had two facelifts by other doctors before she met him, but Alex didn't use a single procedure that required a scalpel. He did it all with chemicals and injections and his "secret formulas." The results were remarkable. She lay expectantly on the table while he worked on her, and sat up and looked at him adoringly when he had finished. He had heard his assistants arrive while he was working. He had opened the locked closet in the treatment room and prepared the injections himself. He preferred it that way. He didn't like even his assistants observing the combinations he used.

"Thank you, Alex," she said, as though relieved of a great burden. The agony of age. And then she asked him a question. "How old was that girl you had with you last night?" He smiled when he answered. The treatment he had just performed on Marilyn had gone well. He had found just the right sequence of procedures for her recently, and was pleased with the result. He knew she would be happy with it this time too.

"She's thirty-three, almost thirty-four," he said simply about Michaela.

"She looks like a teenager. What do you use on her? She's a beautiful girl." Marilyn was in awe of her figure and face and her youthful appearance.

"Yes, she is," he agreed, looking vague for a moment, thinking of their hours in the pool the night before, and he forced the images from his mind. "She came to me when she was very young. We've been perfecting her treatments for five years," he said quietly. "It's mostly mesotherapy with a little magic thrown in." Marilyn was an expert and knew that mesotherapy meant injections that combined pharmaceuticals with hormones and enzymes that had been controversial for years and could be dangerous in the wrong hands. But she trusted Alex totally. Alex was a master at it.

"Do you think we should give that a try?" Marilyn had been more willing to be daring ever since she was facing sixty. She knew that her husband had been cheating on her for years, and had a new young mistress in Newport Beach people said he was mad for. She was twenty-two.

"I think we're doing fine with the serum we're using," Alex said seriously. "We can try mesotherapy if you like, but everyone responds to it differently. Michaela has had a particularly good reaction to it, but I really love the effect of what we're doing on you right now." He looked pleased. Many of his clients came to him for simple Botox shots, and

Voluma for their lips, but he had experimented with many other procedures over the years, depending on the patient's needs. He tailored each formula precisely to them, and believed that surgery was never the right answer. Every treatment he gave was chemical.

"I'd like to try laser lipo or body contouring one of these days," Marilyn said, always desperate for a better result in the ongoing fight against weight and age.

"I'm liking cryolipolysis or cool sculpting these days. Michaela, whom you met last night, has done quite a lot of it," he said confidently. "You saw the result." He had no problem attributing Michaela's naturally perfect beauty of body and face to treatments she'd never had.

"Let's do that then." Marilyn had total faith in Alex, as all of his patients did. His Harvard diplomas were proudly displayed on his office wall and inspired confidence. Most of his patients tried anything he suggested. The less adventuresome ones stuck with the tried-and-true procedures they had used for years before they met him. But some, like Marilyn, were desperate enough to try anything, as long as Dr. Alex gave it his blessing or had suggested it.

She picked up her large pink alligator Birkin and gave him a hug as they left the treatment room. He had spent an hour with her, and his office was in full swing when she left. She was delighted with the look of his new offices that her husband had paid for a good part of. Roger did it willingly in order to keep Marilyn happy and off his back. He didn't ask questions, he just wrote the checks.

"How many patients do I have today?" Alex asked his assistant, Wendy. She was Korean, in her mid-thirties, and had a delicately beautiful face and exquisite skin. She'd had extensive work done on her face in Korea and he helped her maintain it as a perk of her job. He loved having beauty all around him.

"You have nine patients today," Wendy said, consulting a list. He liked to see ten or twelve. It gave him time to give special attention to those who needed it. Some were confident and experienced enough to come and go in a few minutes. Others needed to be hand-carried psychologically through the procedures. Each of his patients was special to him and got the support they needed. He had spent a year in another house in Beverly Hills adding to his client list, while he got his new center ready, after he moved from Florida. He had the solid, steady, regular local clientele to support it now. Some women flew in, from Arkansas, Texas, Oklahoma. He had opened Bellissima with infinitely careful planning and forethought. He was well aware too that many of his patients came to him to fix ills and sorrows in their lives that even his treatments and procedures couldn't touch. The psychologically unstable frequently sought the services of plastic surgeons to change things they couldn't cure, unfaithful or lost husbands, disappointing lives, ungrateful children, financial reversals and lost fortunes, and the final cruelties past a certain age or the tragedy of terminal illness. He spent time with his patients before they began their treatments to make sure he didn't miss a loose cannon among them, or someone seriously disturbed. He was extremely vigilant about that, as most plastic surgeons were. And in some cases he asked for a psychiatric evaluation before he would treat them.

Wendy lowered her voice to say something to him the other two women in the office couldn't hear. "I believe you still have a guest upstairs." He smiled.

"I believe you're right. How long until my next patient?" She glanced at her watch.

"Forty minutes. Elizabeth Marcus. She usually comes late." All she did was lips and Botox. He nodded and left the room where they were working on billing. He was making a fortune and had been for the last two years. Before that, he had made a very handsome living in Palm Beach, but it was out in the stratosphere in L.A., mostly by word of mouth thanks to other satisfied patients. And after his ad campaign, it would be at an even higher level.

He headed for the white marble staircase to his apartment, and used the code to let himself in. His patients didn't know that he also lived there, nor did his investors. He had designed the upper floor himself with the developer. It had everything he needed and provided him a huge, very elegant apartment.

Michaela was standing naked in his snow-white living room when he walked in. She looked like a goddess. She turned and looked at him with a smile. She had a bold cheekiness to her that he loved. She wasn't vulgar or arrogant. She was daring and afraid of nothing. She was unusually confident for a girl her age. "Want to go for a swim?" she suggested. He laughed, remembering the erotic delights of the night before.

"I'd love to. But I'm working. I have a patient in forty minutes. No time for a swim now. Later." He hadn't thought when he saw the beautiful pool that he would ever have as much pleasure in it as he had with her. Michaela was an unexpected gift in his life, and like no one else he had ever met. They were a perfect match. He could sense it.

"What would you like to do then?" she asked with a slow smile as she walked toward him, tantalizingly. Unable to wait a moment longer, he lunged toward her, and she ran away from him on light feet, and he chased her through the apartment, while she laughed at him, eluded him, leaping over furniture, and then let him catch her. Sometimes she was a child and he loved it. It made him feel like a boy again. But there was nothing innocent about her. She was knowing and cunning, with a wealth of experience. He'd had many women in his life, had never married, and had lived with a few, but had never known a woman like her and so much like him. She fulfilled all his fantasies as though she read his mind.

She found new ways to fill the next half hour of his time. She said she was going back to her apartment while he went to work, and she had a go-see that afternoon. She wanted to keep her hand in her modeling career even though she was his ambassador now. Her first night out with him had been a huge success. And he wanted her to meet some of his more important patients, to inspire confidence in him from the way she looked. It was a strong subliminal message. He was beginning to think he wouldn't like her going back and forth to her apartment. He liked having her near at hand for the occasional free time he had between patients, she seemed to know so well how to fill it. It was a whole new way of working for him, and he liked it immensely. She was a very creative girl, and a free spirit. And he was beginning to suspect that he could neither control nor possess her. It was a first for him and an aphrodisiac like no other.

*

Billie was just leaving the pathology lab at Cedars at noon to go down to the cafeteria for lunch when her cellphone rang. It was Jason, she was surprised to see.

"Hi, is this a bad time?" he asked her.

"No, I'm just going to lunch. How are you?" She'd had fun with him the night before at their Mexican dinner and after.

"I'm great and I happen to be outside. Can I drag you off campus to a deli I know nearby?" She was startled and didn't know what to say for a second.

"Are you here?" she asked him. "I mean in the neighborhood somewhere?"

"I am. There was a Mafia killing today I had to cover. Very old-style, in a barbershop near the hospital. A rival Mafia family killed three of the top guys. It's all drug-related nowadays." He sounded blasé about it. He had seen the same scenario too many times. "If you go out the main entrance and look to the right, you'll see me. I'm wearing a red shirt." She was almost there and did as he told her. She smiled when she saw him. She was still wearing a lab coat, and someone had left a stethoscope in the pocket, which she didn't need for work.

Jason walked toward her, smiling too, and she looked up into his brown eyes, happy to see him. "The deli is only a block away, do you want to walk?" He was glad he had called her on the off chance she'd be free. He was happy she was.

"Sure. It must be upsetting going to crime scenes like that," she said, walking along beside him, enjoying the sun and his company for lunch. It was an unexpected treat.

"I've gotten used to it, which I don't like either. You get inured and hardened to the horrors of the human condition, and the things people do to each other. I'm definitely ready for a switch to a better department. But I don't know music, or anything about gardening or cooking. I could do art or theater reviews, I guess. But I still want politics," he explained. "I've had all the gang murders I can stomach. How was your work today?"

"Interesting. I'm learning a lot." She loved the feeling that she was acquiring knowledge she could use later.

They had gotten to the deli by then, and it smelled delicious when they walked in. The smell of wholesome food reminded Billie instantly of her mother.

"My mom used to make great soups, especially in winter." Billie ordered a cup of turkey noodle soup, to honor the memory. And a turkey sandwich to go with it, with cranberry sauce on freshly made whole wheat bread. "My mother was a really good cook. I'm sorry I never learned how, the year that I took care of my sister and my father. We ate a lot of hamburgers and frozen pizza. My sister can't cook either. But she never eats so she doesn't care. The last time I looked there was half a lemon and three Coke Zeros in our fridge. I buy takeout on the way home."

"I actually like to cook," Jason said. "My mom's not much of a cook either. I learned in self-defense. I'll cook dinner for you some night when we both have time. I make great spaghetti and meatballs, and steak." He had ordered a pastrami sandwich, which was one of the deli's specialties, and a big slab of cheesecake for dessert. He looked very athletic and had a hearty appetite, and he ate all of it while they were talking. He was curious about her sister, the model, and the relationship they shared. Billie seemed like a whole different kind of woman, honest, smart, and straightforward. There was no artifice about her, and he liked her small, delicate, feminine appearance.

"She's off and running with her new guy, the one I told you about," she said about Mickie. "He's a big-deal plastic surgeon, who isn't a surgeon, in Beverly Hills." She laughed. "He only does noninvasive treatments. She's very excited about it, and about him. I don't know anything about plastic surgery. It always seems kind of narcissistic to me."

"As long as she's not involved with a drug dealer, that's good. There are a lot of bad guys in L.A. who prey on pretty, innocent young women, actresses and models. I see the end result sometimes." He was serious as he said it, and Billie nodded. The plastic surgeon sounded showy to her, but at least he was a serious professional man.

"My sister is pretty and young, but I wouldn't call her innocent. She was a grown-up when she was twelve, or acted like one. I used to worry about her, especially after my mom died, but she can take care of herself. And she goes nuts about a guy for a while, but then she gets bored, and drops him and moves on. And the plastic surgeon is too old for her. He's forty-two. He won't last long either. She's nineteen and very adult for her age. She's still young, but pretty jaded." It surprised Jason, because there was a natural quality and an innocence about Billie that he found very attractive, and made him want to protect her. The two women sounded very different.

"It's weird how different siblings can be," Billie said as she ate her sandwich. She loved the food at the deli where Jason had taken her. He liked to eat well. "My sister used to joke and say she'd been switched at the hospital at birth and didn't belong in our family. But she and our father have a lot in common." She didn't add that they were both only interested in themselves. She hadn't spoken to her father in months. She didn't call him anymore. He never sounded pleased to hear from her, and didn't care about what she said, or what she was doing. She'd sent him a text when she got to L.A., just so he'd know where she was, and said she was staying with Mickie. There had been no response. He had felt no responsibility for her whatsoever as soon as she turned eighteen and left for college. He considered his job done, even though she had no other parent, with her mother gone. She knew that Mickie called him once in a while, and he was happy to hear from her. They were kindred spirits, and neither of them expected much from the other, which made it easy for him. He had his dairy and his bottle of bourbon at night, and that was all he needed. An occasional call from Mickie was icing on the cake, but he didn't need anyone in his life, not even her. And Mickie was much the same. She had never mourned their mother as Billie had, and never talked about her. Billie still missed her five years later.

"My sister and I are somewhat different, but not that much," Jason said. "She loves country life, I prefer the city. But we both write, she her novels, and I for the paper. Our parents instilled a love of writing and books in us all our lives."

"My mom used to read voraciously. I don't think my father and sister have read a book in their lives. She says she's too busy living life to want to read about it. I guess that's one way to look at it. All my mom wanted was for me to get a good education. She would have been thrilled that I went to MIT. I couldn't believe it when I got in, with a full scholarship. My school counselor really went to bat for me." Listening to her, Jason felt faintly guilty, as he always did, for the easy childhood and youth he had had, going to the best private schools and great colleges, with enthusiastic and unfailing support from his parents. He was always deeply grateful to them now that he realized how terrific they had been, and he enjoyed spending time with them when he went back to New York. He tried to get back a few times a year. It was harder to get to Vermont to see his sister, in the small town where she lived. They spent holidays together in Connecticut with their parents since neither of them was married or had kids.

"Do you like sports?" Jason asked Billie, wanting to get to know her better.

"You mean playing them, or as a spectator?" she asked him with a mischievous look.

"Both. I play a lot of squash and tennis, and was crazy about basketball and baseball as a kid, and football too. I wanted to be a professional basketball or baseball player when I was in school. I play on a baseball team at the paper, and I love going to games. Do you like baseball?" He looked hopeful when he asked. He was a rabid Dodgers fan. And he went to Lakers games whenever he could.

"I like it a lot," she said. "I like football too. I went to the Harvard games a few times. It was really fun." She was enjoying him too. He just seemed like a happy, well-balanced person. He hadn't had a tormented childhood and didn't hate his parents, which seemed rare. The result was a happy guy who didn't have a chip on his shoulder or a grudge against the world. It made him fun to be around. She hadn't had an easy childhood, but she wasn't angry about it, and she had had unconditional love from her mother until she was seventeen, which had given her a good start, even if she had been alone ever since. The early years had counted for a lot.

"I've got season tickets to the Dodgers. If you like, you can come with me sometime." He usually took one of the reporters he worked with, who were happy to get a free seat at the game.

The hour she had for lunch went by quickly, and he walked her back to the hospital. He had gotten several texts during lunch, and had to go to a trial that afternoon. There was a hostage situation in progress in East L.A. The paper had sent him a text about it, to make him aware, but they had sent others to cover the story who were in the area at the time and could get there faster. There was always a story breaking somewhere. There was no lack of crime in L.A.

"Thanks for the nice lunch," she said to him when they got to the hospital. "It was an unexpected treat."

"I'm all over the city. I'll text you when I'm in the neighborhood next time and we can do it again." He smiled at her. "And I'll see you at the apartment. Maybe we can go for a swim one night after work. I'll call you for the next Dodgers game," he promised. There was a lot to look forward to. She waved as she disappeared into the building, and he walked to where he had left his car, looking pleased. Their lunch together had been even better than he'd hoped. And he couldn't wait to take her to a Dodgers game.

Alex had three patients for simple Botox shots that day, two of them with Voluma for their lips, which was his preferred brand. The treatments were easy to administer and the patients were young and starting early. All three of them were under thirty and wanting to stop the signs of age before they started.

He had a patient for Thermage that afternoon, which used radiofrequency energy and had longer-lasting results than some of the other treatments. He was using it on a patient for the third time, and she loved it, although it was more painful than most of his protocols. He did a collagen thread lift after that, which required steady hands to inject the tiny threads loaded with collagen under the skin along the jawline. As the collagen was released over time, it

119

appeared to lift the patient's face almost like a facelift, and you could see the results within days.

He finished the afternoon with a laser liposuction patient to dissolve fat around the patient's face and neck. It was one of the more expensive treatments he administered and like all of them required skill and experience. It was less invasive than normal liposuction, which required the removal of fat with a tube and could be dangerous and cause life-threatening infections. With laser lipo the body naturally eliminated the fat, so there was less risk of complications or infection. All of his patients that afternoon were back for repeat treatments, and had been ecstatic with their results the first time. Alex loved working on the women he knew well, who were well versed in what to expect. The fearful, anxious first-timers were sweet but it took a lot longer to deal with them, to allay their fears. He was wonderful with his patients. They all loved him and trusted him completely.

The proofs of the photographs for his ad campaign came in that afternoon. He was using them for a brochure too, listing and explaining all the different services he offered, like a menu for patients to choose from, to make it simpler for them by explaining the procedures.

The photos of Mickie were fabulous. He picked one for his first ad immediately, and for the front of the brochure, and he loved the before and after. He was going to put them in the brochure. He ordered all of it, and showed the proofs to Mickie when she came to his apartment that night. She sat staring at the before and after for a long time.

"Shit, I hope I don't look like that at forty. Can you do anything to prevent that, starting now?"

"Not at nineteen, my love. We can talk about it in ten or fifteen years, depending on how your face holds up." It didn't bother her for a minute that the photographs they were using were dishonest, that the photograph of her as she looked now was not an "after," but very much a "before." And the fact that the before photo was a total lie no longer even occurred to her as she studied how her hair looked. She didn't confront Alex about it. He was fine with it too. As far as he was concerned, the ads were a form of art, and whatever he and Mickie did was part of the artistic process. It would make his patients happy in the end and reassure them that they would get fabulous results too, just like Mickie. The pure dishonesty of it didn't bother either of them. The end justified the means in their minds. They were reassuring patients of the quality of service, and promising great results that Alex was sure he could deliver.

He told her they were going to a film premiere on Friday night, and asked her to buy another fabulous dress, and gave her his credit card to do so. He felt comfortable doing that now. Several times that week, she came to the office and met his patients. She was warm and fun and lively, and helped the new patients relax before they went in for their treatments. Seeing Mickie and believing she was thirty-three made them ready to leap onto the treatment table if they would wind up with results like hers. She played the part of ambassador well, and Alex was proud of her and happy he had hired her. So was Mickie. She loved being around him, and when he had a break between patients, he would open one of the supply closets with his code, and they would have sex between the shelves, being mindful not to break any bottles or do any damage.

Mickie had never had as much fun in her life as she was having with Alex. She was on top of the world with him. The movie premiere on Friday exceeded her wildest expectations. They walked the red carpet, and were photographed continuously, Alex in one of his designer tuxedos and Mickie in a black sequined dress that molded her body like shimmering lava. They were in the Style section of the paper the next day. They were becoming the it couple, and had broken the sound barrier into the Hollywood set that Alex wanted access to.

He had placed ads in *People, Vogue, Harper's Bazaar, Vanity Fair,* and *Entertainment Weekly,* online and on all the newsstands. Mickie's face was everywhere and she looked incredible. She was as ecstatic as Alex about the press they were getting. And her modeling agency liked it too.

Jason asked Billie about it on Saturday, as they lay on deck chairs at the pool at their building. Mickie hadn't been home all week. She was staying at Alex's apartment, and texted Billie that she was fine.

Jason showed Billie a photo of her at the movie premiere, and asked about it. The caption said "Renowned plastic surgeon Dr. Alex Addison with model Michaela Banks, the iconic face of his new nonsurgical esthetic center Bellissima," and the photograph showed them on the red carpet with Mickie in the black sequined skintight gown. She looked like a black mermaid in it.

"Is that your sister, Mickie?" Jason asked her. Billie glanced at the photograph and nodded.

"Yeah, that's her." She read the caption and could see why her sister hadn't been to the apartment all week. She was obviously having fun with her super doctor.

"She's a knockout," Jason said clinically, but Mickie wasn't the kind of woman who appealed to him at all. Physical perfection, but she looked like she had no soul. All beauty and no heart. He thought her expression was ice cold, unlike Billie, who was warm, bubbly, and fun, and pretty too, in a natural way. She wasn't a stunner like Mickie, but she was real. He knew Michaela's type and had dated a few of them, but not for long. He much preferred Billie sitting next to him, with her hair piled up in a banana clip, in her faded blue bathing suit from high school, and her almost adolescent body. She looked like a little elf to him sometimes, and she had the innocence of youth and honesty in her eyes. Her sister was all woman, and there wasn't a shred of innocence about her. She looked like she knew exactly what she was doing at all times. There was no naivete there. She was a pro. Her flawless beauty held no lure for him.

"She must be having fun. That's the doctor. She works for him now, as an ambassador," Billie said without a hint of jealousy. She was happy for her sister. "That's the life she's always wanted, ever since she was a kid. I'm glad if she's getting what she wants." It wasn't the life she wanted, but she wished her sister well. Billie had a generous spirit.

"I probably have a missing chromosome or something, but I don't find women like that sexy at all. There's no softness there, no heart. Is she like that in person? So perfect and sophisticated, I mean?"

"Totally," Billie said without criticism. "Mickie knows exactly what she wants, and she goes for it, and always gets it. She's been like that since she was five. She had my father totally under her spell from the minute she could talk, and everyone else. She was a rotten little kid and I got blamed for everything she did, as I told you, but she's a lot nicer now." Jason doubted it, but didn't say so. The look on Michaela's face wasn't nice, in his opinion. There was no sweetness there at all.

"Is she in love with the doctor?" He was curious.

"I don't know. I doubt it. She never is. And she only met him recently. But he's a way to get where she wants to go. He's awfully old for her to fall in love with. I don't think Mickie's ever been in love, except maybe with herself." It was an astute observation, and accurate. She was a classic narcissist. And Jason was much happier with the other sister. He doubted that he would like Mickie if he ever met her. Billie hadn't suggested it since the night of their first date and didn't intend to again. She instinctively sensed that they wouldn't like each other. And Mickie would never make the effort to meet a friend of her sister's. Billie was curious about the doctor and would have liked to meet him, but she knew Mickie would never let that happen.

They both swam for a while, and went to their respective apartments to dress for the Dodgers game Jason was taking her to that night. She was looking forward to it, and they had a ball when they got there. He had very good seats, behind home plate, with an unobstructed view. Jason bought hot dogs, popcorn, sodas, fries, and eventually ice cream, and it was a good game against the San Francisco

Giants. The Dodgers had been on a winning streak and Jason was ecstatic when they won. Billie had loved it, and they wound up back at the pool at the apartment for a late-night swim. She was lying on the deck chair, drying off afterward, looking up at a starry sky, when he sat down on the edge of her chair, leaned down and gently kissed her, and she responded and pulled him closer. He lay on the chair next to her, overwhelmed with desire for her. It had been a perfect day for both of them. They hadn't known each other for long, but he already had the feeling that he knew her well, and he liked everything about her, and he found her petite, graceful body incredibly sexy. He was constantly aware that he wanted to protect her, but he didn't know from what. There were no evils lurking, but she brought out the best in him. His life was pleasant before, but he had been happier ever since he met her.

They kissed for a long time, cautiously exploring each other's bodies, and he whispered to her. "Do you want to come to my place?" he asked her. She didn't want to suggest hers, it was so starkly furnished, and everything in it was battered and ugly. Mickie had wasted neither time nor money decorating it, and his place would inevitably be better.

They walked up the stairs to his apartment, not rushing, savoring the moment, hand in hand. He opened the door with his key, and she immediately saw the warm atmosphere he had created, with vintage furniture, a big brown leather couch, comfortable overstuffed chairs, and cozy fabrics. It had the feel of a western country home, with a touch of Santa Fe. It looked like a Ralph Lauren ad, which suited him, casual but made up of elements of quality, and his bedroom was masculine but inviting, in beige and navy, with a big cozy plaid blanket on the bed. He carefully laid her on it as they peeled off their wet bathing suits and dropped them on the floor, and he gently made love to her with mounting passion. He reached a crescendo more rapidly than he intended, but he wanted her so badly and found her so irresistibly feminine and appealing that he couldn't hold back for long, although he was an artful lover. She'd never made love feeling that way before, compared to her loveless, fumbling, beer-driven college experiences that had never stirred any emotion in her other than embarrassment afterward. Making love with Jason was entirely different, and although they had only met recently, she already knew she was falling in love with him, and so was he with her. She was the woman he had been waiting for and didn't know it. And he felt jubilant as he lay in bed with her, and looked at her afterward with a broad smile.

"You are the most wonderful woman I have ever met," he said, and kissed her, and held her tight for a minute and then looked down at her again. She had a dreamy-eyed expression, still in the after haze of their lovemaking.

"It's never been like that for me with anyone," she said, still surprised. But he was a dozen years older than the inexperienced boys she had slept with, and a practiced lover, and it made a difference. The feelings he already had for her made it different for him than it was with the women he had met at bars or parties or at work, where sex was a weekend activity, like a sport, with no emotion, only physical skill or prowess. He almost expected to get a score from them when it was over, or ask who won. He never felt that he did. They were never the right women for him, but this little elf of a woman from a dairy farm in Iowa was the one he had been looking for.

They talked late into the night, now that they had found each other, made love again, and she slept in his apartment. She woke up the next morning with the sun streaming into the room, as he began making love to her to wake her up. He had been watching her sleep for an hour and couldn't wait a moment longer to make love to her again. It was an exquisite way to wake up, and afterward they dozed for a little longer and took a shower together, and then he made a big country breakfast of fried eggs, sausages, and bacon. She made toast and burned it and he didn't care. Sitting in his apartment with him, over breakfast, talking and laughing and telling him stories about taking care of the cows, she felt as though she had come home at last. His apartment was twice the size of hers, and she felt totally at ease. He made her feel comfortable, and safe, which was an unfamiliar feeling for her. She had been fighting her own battles for years, defending and protecting herself from her father, her sister, the mean girls at school, and in Jason's world there were no dangers, no predators.

"There's someone I want you to meet," she said when they finished breakfast.

"Your sister?" He wasn't looking forward to it, but didn't say so.

"No, you'll meet her at some point when she comes to pick something up at the apartment. I want you to meet my friend Tom Carter when he comes back from his mission in the Middle East. He's like a brother to me, and you two would love each other."

"You two never had a romance?" Jason asked, curious about Tom. She had mentioned him several times when talking about her childhood.

"Never. He was my family. He and my mom." Her father had been a disinterested bystander. And her sister had been the enemy for most of it, even if the war was over now.

"I look forward to meeting him," he said warmly. "And I want you to meet my family. They will love you," he said with assurance. They had been good about never bugging him about why he didn't have a serious woman in his life. At thirty-three, they didn't think there was any rush. His sister was thirty-five now, and they hadn't bothered her either. They figured it would happen at the right time when the right person came along. His sister had finally met her man two years before, and was happy living with him, with no plans for marriage, which was fine with his parents too. Jason had an idea about when he wanted Billie to meet them but it was too soon to say anything. He was just enjoying the wonders they had discovered the night before, and looking forward to more of them as they got to know each other better.

That night, they went back to their own apartments, and lasted about an hour. Jason called her and she answered, wide awake, lying in the dark in her bed, thinking about him.

"I can't sleep without you," he said in a husky voice, and she smiled.

"Me too. I was thinking about you, and last night."

"Will you come back now?" he asked her, sounding boyish and sexy, and she laughed.

"See you in two minutes." She hopped out of bed, slipped her feet into slippers, locked her door and ran up the stairs to his apartment on the floor above. He was holding the door open for her in his boxers, and she was wearing an old cotton nightgown. He smiled as soon as he saw her.

"Welcome home," he said as he kissed her, swept her into his arms as though she were weightless, carried her to his bed, and laid her there. The boxers and the old cotton nightgown lay on the floor seconds later.

Chapter 7

As Billie had predicted, Jason met Mickie one evening when she showed up at the apartment. Jason had picked Billie up after work in his Jeep, they had gotten sushi and were going to eat in his kitchen. Billie went to get some more of her textbooks she wanted to study, and Jason was with her when Mickie suddenly appeared like a vision. She was surprised to see them, and immediately turned a sexy look toward Jason. It wasn't personal, Billie knew, it was just the way Mickie responded whenever she saw a male between the ages of thirteen and ninety-seven. She couldn't help it. It was how she was wired. Jason could sense that too.

"Sorry, I won't stay long," she said to Billie, curious who the man was. He was nice-looking. She would text her about it later. Billie was digging through a box of books when she walked in, and Jason was waiting for her, sprawled on the uncomfortable couch. He stood up when Mickie walked in, as a reflex more than anything else, and she noticed how tall and well-built he was. He looked like he worked out a lot, which was true. Alex was leaner, thinner, less athletic, though he had a trainer twice a week, and he wasn't as tall as Jason. He was an entirely different style. Jason looked a little too wholesome for Mickie, which Billie knew too. "I just came by to pick up my bikinis and beachwear," she said to Billie. "Alex is going to see a patient in Hawaii to do some treatments, and I'm going with him." She was starting to take the perks of his lifestyle for granted, expecting them as the norm, as though they were her due.

"Lucky you," Billie said, and introduced Jason to her sister. She saw an odd look pass between them, of hostility and suspicion. It was fleeting and vanished just as quickly as it had appeared.

"I've heard a lot about you," Jason said pleasantly, trying to observe the usual norms of introduction to a family member of the person one was dating.

"Probably all bad," Mickie said easily. "She lies," she added, and disappeared into the bedroom, as Billie stacked up the books she was looking for.

Mickie was back five minutes later with two well-stuffed garbage bags and two valises. The garbage bags were visibly full of hats to wear at the pool. "Alex sees patients all over the place. We were in Palm Springs last weekend, and we're going to see an actress he's treating in Montecito." She was clearly trying to impress them and Jason took an immediate and profound dislike to her. He had the feeling that she was trying to make Billie look and feel bad in front of her new man. Mickie couldn't help herself, she was a scorpion to her core and needed to sting someone in order to feel good about herself.

"It must be fun for you to tag along," Jason said indifferently, reminding her subtly that she was just an add-on, not the main event. She was there for decoration and not much else. And he didn't like the supercilious way she looked at Billie, who was worth a thousand of her sister, a million in his opinion. He had a visceral reaction of dislike for Mickie, and she had excellent antennae and could sense it, and didn't like him either.

"How did you two meet?" she asked, pretending to be interested and lingering for a moment to ask.

"At the pool here," Billie said innocently. She knew her sister better than that, but she was out of practice dealing with her sister's games. It had been a while.

"That's nice for both of you, convenient," Mickie said

with a supercilious look. She was the star now, and they were two poor inconsequential people far beneath her. "Have fun, you two, see ya," she said, and sailed out the door, juggling her suitcases and the garbage bags. Feeling intentionally rude, Jason didn't offer to help her. She didn't deserve it. The door banged behind her and Billie exchanged a look with him.

"I don't like your sister," he said in a tense tone. "I'm sorry to be so blunt. I don't like the way she treats you, or the way she talks to you."

"I don't pay attention to it anymore," Billie said quietly and stood up with her books in her arms. "She's young, and she feels like hot stuff with her fancy doctor in Bel Air. When that ends, she'll just be one of the masses again." But there was a hard look in Mickie's eyes that Jason found almost frightening. There was ice in her veins. It was hard to believe that the two women were even related. Billie locked the door behind them and he carried the books back to his apartment for her. She was sleeping there every night now, and it was comforting to walk into his cozy, inviting apartment after the brief visit to her barren, ugly one. Mickie's behavior hadn't shocked her as much as it did Jason. Billie had seen her behave much worse at other times. They had no fight with each other. Billie didn't begrudge her the fun she was having, or her moment of stardom in the press on Alex's arm. She was happy for Mickie. Her dreams were coming true. But Jason sensed something truly evil about her. It made him nervous thinking of her anywhere near Billie. As he had suspected, from what Billie said about her, and the photograph he'd seen of her in the paper, she was a woman without a heart, and possibly some seriously scary agendas. In his mind she was using the fancy Bel Air doctor for her own purposes as much as he was using her as the face of his beauty center. In Jason's book, they deserved each other, two users exploiting each other. He felt sorry for Billie being related to someone like her. She deserved a lot better than that. She was a warm, kind, intelligent, honest woman. He found it amazing that anyone as young as Mickie could already be so twisted and ambitious at such an early age. Billie seemed like an innocent next to her. Jason didn't think that she fully saw her sister as evil, as he thought she potentially could be if it served her purposes. And the very thought of it frightened him for Billie, and chilled him to the bone.

By August, two months after Alex had opened Bellissima, he was seeing ten or twelve patients a day. They had people waiting two months for appointments to see him, and he was invited away by patients every weekend, to do treatments at their beach and country homes. Many of them sent their planes to pick him up, and Mickie went everywhere with him. She had met all his most important patients by then. They were out almost every night, at all the best parties in L.A. He had become the darling of the Hollywood set. He was still running the beautiful ads in all the major magazines, and Mickie had been asked to do fashion shoots identifying her by name in *Vogue* and *Vanity Fair*. She went to fewer go-sees now. Clients of her agency called and asked for her. She was becoming a celebrity in her own right, which meant a lot to her. It had always been one of her dreams, to be famous. And it was starting to happen. She and Alex were frequently in the press. Her before and after photos were in the Bellissima brochure. His patients still marveled at the way she looked for her age, when he confidentially shared with them that she had just turned thirty-four, which he claimed was the best-kept secret in the world. But he was telling them so they could evaluate how effective his work and secret formulas had been on her. He still managed to keep an aura of secrecy around Bellissima, as it nestled in the rarefied atmosphere of Bel Air.

In August, as they came back from a weekend in Atherton, just outside San Francisco, at the home of the brightest young billionaire star of Silicon Valley, he and Mickie had frantic sex in the bathroom of the plane. They were alone on the flight with the crew, and he asked Mickie to move in with him.

"You're using your old apartment as a closet. Why don't you just move it all to my place, and give your sister the apartment? You don't need it." Mickie hadn't spent a night there in two months, and she loved the idea of fully living with him. She knew that she had used her own particular brand of magic on him, and he was seriously addicted to her, and couldn't go more than a dozen hours without having sex with her. It had become a desperate need for him. They had sex at the parties they went to, in the homes of the patients they visited as guests, in stores and restaurants. It had become a game to find the most unusual places and not get caught, and once his office staff left at night, they had sex in every possible position and place in the entire Bellissima Center. Sex had become the most powerful tool Mickie had to control him, and what he loved most about her. He couldn't imagine his life without her, and his patients loved talking to her. They thought her a lovely, very refined, sweet woman who calmed any fears they had before their treatments and sometimes stayed in the room to hold their hands. She was useful to Alex in so many ways. And she knew exactly how to behave in each situation.

Discreet and demure in his office. And the most daring, outrageous, down-and-dirty hellion in his bed.

She moved the last of her wardrobe into his apartment at Bellissima, and she felt very secure once she did. She had told Billie that she would continue to pay her half of the rent until the end of their lease, which was a kindness to Billie. She couldn't have afforded to pay the entire rent, and she didn't want to move in with Jason, even if she was sleeping there every night. They still had the freedom to sleep at their own apartments if they wanted to. She was happy for Mickie that things were working out for her. She never invited Billie over, or offered to introduce her to Alex. She kept her family in the background, and Billie didn't expect anything different from her. Families weren't important to Mickie, nor to Alex, since his parents and grandparents were all dead and he had no siblings. And he had never expressed a desire to meet Mickie's sister since they didn't appear to be close and Mickie had never talked about her.

Mickie was aware that Alex's practice was booming. He charged a fortune for some of the procedures and there were telltale signs that his income was increasing exponentially. He bought himself an Aston Martin, which had always been his dream. He chartered planes when his patients didn't send theirs for him. He no longer flew commercial, and he was always generous with Mickie, and had bought her several pretty pieces of jewelry from Van Cleef and Cartier. Two bracelets and a necklace, no engagement ring yet, but Mickie wouldn't be surprised if it happened. He said he couldn't live without her now, and she believed him. And she enjoyed his lifestyle immensely, and kept him sexually satisfied no matter what it took to please him and live out his fantasies. No woman had ever been as willing and creative as she was. He got anxious if she left the house for more than a few hours. He was obsessed with her. It was all-consuming, and all he could think of day and night. Even when he was working, he thought of what he would do with her in a few hours. Nothing was too outrageous for her, or off limits. He'd never known any woman like her.

Alex and Mickie spent Labor Day weekend at the home of patients in Mexico, and on the flight back on Monday, he told her that they had an important dinner engagement on Tuesday night. He emphasized that it was important, and didn't tell her with whom. She never asked questions. He told her what to wear. He didn't tell her that he had rented a private room at Chateau Marmont until that afternoon. He told her to wear something serious and sexy, on the more conservative side, for the dinner. He looked intense when he said it, and added that it was a business meeting and he wanted her with him. It was an important opportunity that would affect his business in future. He mentioned casually that if it went well, he was thinking of leasing a jet for their use, so they could travel to see patients anywhere in the U.S. at any time. He had just turned forty-three and he was already a very rich man. Things had gone well for him ever since he opened Bellissima and he called Mickie his lucky charm.

They left Bel Air at seven, and were at the restaurant by seven-fifteen. Alex employed two security guards at all times at the house now, and one of them drove them in a Bentley Alex had recently bought. He let Mickie drive it whenever she wanted, and she had dropped by to see Billie at work to show it off. She didn't like going to see Billie at the apartment. She didn't want to run into Jason. Their mutual dislike was palpable whenever their paths crossed, so she avoided him whenever possible, and she didn't see Billie often. Their lives were very different now. Mickie's star had risen high into the heavens at rocket speed in the last three months, thanks to Alex. But once in a while, she liked to see Billie just to show her how far she'd come and rub it in. Her wardrobe was no longer secondhand. It was all brand-new. Billie was happy for her.

Alex's guests arrived at the restaurant at seven-thirty, and Mickie saw that Alex had rented a double room. There was an anteroom for cocktails, and a space beyond it for dinner. Three Asian men arrived looking like serious businessmen. They looked at Mickie with interest, and spoke to Alex in low voices. Two of them spoke fluent English, and they translated for the third. She heard Alex say something about Korea at some point, so they were obviously Korean.

Mickie had no idea what the meeting was about, but from what Alex had said, there was a great deal of money involved.

The three men spoke with Alex in low voices over cocktails before dinner. All three of them and Alex drank Scotch, and Alex had ordered very high-priced French wines with dinner. None of them ever spoke to Mickie during the evening. She was there purely as decoration or, she wondered, as an example of Alex's work, if he told them that she was thirty-three or -four. She was used to people thinking that was her age now, and she thought it was funny. Now and then she acted her age, but usually only with Alex at night. The rest of the time she was believable as being in her thirties, and her wardrobe added to that impression, since the clothes he paid for were so obviously expensive from the most expensive brands.

There was a very intense quality to the meeting, and Mickie had never seen Alex as serious. There was clearly a lot on the line. When the evening had ended, Mickie couldn't tell from Alex's expression if it had gone well or not. He looked exhausted. He didn't speak in the Bentley on the way home, and she asked him gently as they got undressed, "How do you think it went?"

"I can't tell. They spoke among themselves a lot. They play it very close to the vest. They said they'd let me know by the end of the week." They stayed close to the house all day on Saturday and lay by the pool, still waiting for a call.

His cellphone rang at six o'clock on Saturday, and he grabbed it and walked into the house. He sat down in the living room they used as a waiting room to take the call. They were alone in the house. Mickie didn't follow Alex inside. He had been very subdued since the night before, and they had made love only that morning. He was too distracted to even want to have sex with her again after that, which he usually would.

He was on the phone for a long time, and came back to the pool looking dazed. He sat down facing her, and a slow smile lit up his face. His electric blue eyes that his patients talked about were dancing.

"They're in," he told Mickie. He was shaking. "They're

giving me ten million dollars to set up a center like Bellissima in Dallas. They want it up and running in six months. We really do need a plane now, if I'm going to be commuting to Dallas. I haven't figured out how that will work yet," since no one did the treatments except him, or knew the formulas he used. It was all kept secret even from his medical assistants. "But ten million dollars." It really was his dream come true. "And if they're happy with that one, they'll give me another ten to set one up in New York."

"And you'll be giving treatments in all three locations?" She looked incredulous.

"I'll have to figure it out," he said slowly. "We'll have to see how it works in Dallas first. It will be a good test market. I have clients from there who will help us line up the patients." He named a few. "I'll have to do three days in each city. Or four and two. We'll need to work out a system. But ten million dollars, Mickie. Imagine it. We've grown exponentially." And then he thought of something he hadn't asked her before. "When are you going back to Stanford? When I met you, you said you were going back in January. Are you still planning to do that?" He looked anxious about it. "I really need you here, close to me. There's going to be a lot going on." She looked pensive as she considered it.

"I guess I could put it off till the fall semester a year from now," she said, as though it was a major sacrifice for her. She knew just how to play him, and didn't hesitate to do so. He walked to his desk then, took out a checkbook, and wrote a check, walked back, and handed it to her. It was a hundred-thousand-dollar check made out to her.

"Will that help make the decision easier?" he asked her, and she smiled at him. He knew the way to her heart. For him it was sex, for Mickie, it was money. They were an even match.

"I think that will do it. Stanford can wait." She beamed at him, and he pulled her into his arms and fondled her breasts. She never wore her bikini tops, and most of the time they swam or lay in the sun naked.

"Thank you for giving up school for me," he said in a voice already husky with passion. He wasn't sure which excited him more, the Korean investors or Mickie's body.

"How soon will you have to start working on the Dallas center?" she asked him.

"It can wait a while. We'll be able to put it together pretty quickly. But I think I'll lease the plane now," he said. He had other plans in mind, but he wanted to surprise her.

She was leading a golden life with him. The modeling job she had done for him for his ads and the brochure was the best thing that had ever happened to her.

They went upstairs to their bedroom to celebrate. They could both see new horizons opening up. It was a lot to think about, and the treats Mickie had reserved for him drove even the Korean investors and his plans for the Dallas office from his mind.

Billie and Jason were at a Dodgers game that night. He was making an avid baseball fan out of her, and she loved going to the games with him. She was happy with Jason. They both worked hard at their jobs, and enjoyed their time off together. They had a weekend off, and he took her to San Francisco. They stayed at the Fairmont on Nob Hill, and went to all the best restaurants and walked around the city. They crossed the Golden Gate Bridge and drove around Marin County in the car he'd rented. Billie had fun with him. He asked her to move in with him, and it was tempting because she wasn't using her apartment anymore. She agreed and gave the building notice on Monday when they got back. Their relationship seemed more solid now. She moved the few things she had into his apartment that week, and texted Mickie to ask permission to get rid of the furniture. There was nothing worth keeping. It was all battered, stained, and ugly. It had been all Mickie could afford at the time. Now she was shopping regularly at Chanel, and using the credit card Alex had given her almost daily. He didn't seem to care what she spent as long as she looked fabulous and chic all the time. She was a walking advertisement for him, and she had to look spectacular whenever patients would see her. They were still going to parties every night, and walking the red carpet at every event they went to. Mickie was becoming a celebrity in her own right now. People recognized her in stores and in the street, and she'd had an offer to do ads for a perfume campaign. Alex wanted her to do it. She was linked to Bellissima, and he wanted her to get her face out there. Inevitably, it would bring in more patients who wanted to look like her. But Mickie's beauty was a gift of nature, it wasn't man-made or even enhanced by any of Alex's treatments.

She was on the cover of *Us* magazine, on their beauty issue, with the caption "the most beautiful face in the world." Jason saw it at the checkout stand at the supermarket, and Billie put it in their basket.

"I'm happy for her," she said to Jason. He didn't see how. From everything she had told him, Mickie had ruined Billie's youth and childhood. But Billie seemed to forgive her whatever sins she had committed in the past. She had a generous nature, which amazed him.

When Thanksgiving rolled around, neither Mickie nor Billie went home to Iowa. They hadn't in several years, without their mother, and their father didn't care. He hated all holidays since his wife's death and hadn't liked them much before. It was his late wife who had seen to it that they had real holidays. So neither Mickie nor Billie went home for Thanksgiving anymore, only for Christmas, which their father grudgingly acknowledged, but wasn't enthusiastic about either. He hated holidays in general, after his own hard childhood. His parents had died young and he'd been brought up by relatives who beat him regularly and were drunks. Now he was one too.

Alex and Mickie spent the Thanksgiving holiday with favorite patients in Aspen. Jason had to work, so Billie offered to work that day too, so someone else could be with their family. It was a sacrifice she was willing to make. They bought a prepared turkey dinner that night on the way home and ate it in Jason's kitchen. There was a new tenant in her old apartment by then. It was nice being just the two of them, even if they didn't have a big fancy dinner or family to be with. Billie didn't hear from Mickie. She called her father, and he didn't answer the phone. She assumed he was either drunk or having a Thanksgiving meal with friends.

Jason asked her a question, while they each had a slice of pumpkin pie with vanilla ice cream.

"What do you usually do on Christmas?" he asked her. It was clear that she didn't have strong family ties, and she wasn't in regular contact with her father. Jason had called his own family from work that day. His sister and her boyfriend were with his parents when he spoke to them. He was sorry to miss the Thanksgiving holiday with them, but he was going home for Christmas in Connecticut.

"I go home to Iowa, and so does Mickie. I don't know what she's doing this year with Alex. Neither of us had serious boyfriends before, so we went home to spend it with my father. I'm not sure he cares. He doesn't like Christmas, or any holiday. It was more my mother's thing than his," she said quietly.

"Would you come to New York with me?" he asked her. "We spend the actual holiday at my parents' house in Connecticut, and my sister and her boyfriend will come down from Vermont. It's very cozy and informal. I'd love you to come with me, Billie," he said gently. He'd been planning to ask her for months, if they were still together in December. They'd been dating for six months and it had turned into a serious relationship. "My parents would love to meet you. I've never taken anyone home for Christmas before, so it's kind of a big deal," he admitted with a boyish grin. "This will be Thad's second Christmas with us, with my sister. I guess we're all finally growing up." It sounded like a serious invitation to Billie.

"I'd love to come," she said, "but I feel like I should ask

my father how he feels about it. I haven't seen him all year, since last Christmas."

"Does he ever call you?" She never mentioned it. She shook her head.

"No, he doesn't. As you know, we've never been close, particularly since my mother's been gone. But I think I should ask him." It felt like the right thing to do, and Jason respected her for it. "I'll ask Mickie what her plans are too. Thank you for asking me." It meant a lot to her, and it did to him too.

They spent a relaxed weekend watching football and went for a walk on the beach. He'd been busy at work lately—they'd been giving him investigative assignments, some of which were interesting, and he was good at them. It was like solving mysteries. He had come up with some very interesting material that had led to an arrest in one case, and the exposure of a sex trafficking ring coming in from Mexico in another. They were challenging and he liked working on them, more than reporting gang murders.

Billie called Mickie on Monday when she got back from Aspen, and asked her about Christmas.

"Are you going home?" Billie asked her, and Mickie answered quickly.

"Not this year. Alex chartered a boat. We're picking it up in St. Barts, and we're going to float around for two heavenly weeks. We might invite some patients over New Year's." It never dawned on Mickie to invite her sister, and Billie had never met Alex. Mickie had no interest in introducing him to her family. She kept her two lives separate, and Alex had never asked to meet Billie. Jason had commented that they behaved like aliens from another planet. None of the traditional behaviors seemed to apply to them. They each lived in their own bubble, and everything was motivated by Alex's practice. Normal people didn't behave that way in Jason's world. His family meant a great deal to him and they were close. They spoke to each other regularly on the phone, and he admired them and wanted a life like theirs eventually.

"Are you going home?" Mickie asked her. It occurred to Billie that it would be even worse than usual without her sister, not that Mickie made any great effort for the holiday, and nor did her father. But at least they were together. This year she would be alone with her father, which would be very hard. He would be uncommunicative by day, and drunk every night. He and Billie had nothing to say to each other.

"I don't know," Billie said to her sister. "I wanted to ask you about your plans, and I think I'll ask Dad how he feels about it."

"You should just do what you want. Dad doesn't care about Christmas." It was depressing but true. "He can have dinner with friends if he wants to." The truth was that he got excited if Mickie came home, but never about Billie. He hardly spoke to her the whole time she was there. She wondered where her friend Tom would be this Christmas. She hadn't heard from him in a year, on his undercover missions. She missed him, but not as much now that she had Jason.

"Jason invited me to spend Christmas with his family in New York and Connecticut, but I didn't want to leave you and Dad in the lurch." It had never occurred to Mickie to ask Billie about her plans, and it surprised her to hear Billie say it. She was excited about the boat Alex had chartered. It was huge.

Billie called her father that night, and he sounded like he'd been drinking when he answered. He wasn't incoherent but he was slurring a little. Any later, and he would have been passed out. There was a very narrow window of opportunity to talk to him at night.

"Hi, Dad, how've you been?" she said in as cheerful a voice as she could muster. Calling him always depressed her. It brought up painful memories for her, of being ignored all her life, being considered a freak, and being dismissed.

"I'm fine. Who is this? Mickie or Billie?" They had similar voices.

"It's Billie," she said.

"Oh. Is something wrong?"

"No, everything's fine. I wanted to say hello, and I wanted to know how you're feeling about Christmas, if you want me to come home."

"I don't care," he said gruffly. "I hate Christmas, you know that. Your mother liked all that nonsense, Santa Claus and Christmas trees. It's a lot of hogwash. Is Mickie coming home?" he asked her.

"I don't think so." It was up to Mickie to tell him. He sounded ancient as she listened to him, and he wasn't. He was in his forties, and he sounded seventy. Hard work and bitterness, alcohol, and losing his wife at an early age had made an old man of him prematurely. He had no love in his heart for anyone, and hadn't been great to Billie's mother either. He was a hard man, and came from a hard family.

"I'm not going to make a fuss about Christmas if you come home," he warned her. He never did. It kind of went on around him, like water around a rock in the stream.

"Would you mind if I don't?" Billie asked him. He didn't make it sound appealing. "I could come another time."

"I don't care. Where are you living now?"

"I'm still in L.A. I got a job here in June, so I stayed." He didn't ask what the job was, and didn't care, as long as she wasn't asking him for money. She never did, and hadn't since she left home for college with her scholarship.

"Are you still living with Mickie?" he asked her.

"No." They were both living with men, and he had no idea. "We're living in separate places. Well, I guess I won't come home then, if it's okay with you." The idea of spending Christmas with him was just too depressing now that she'd spoken to him. She'd spend the whole holiday in her room, waiting to leave, while he drank himself to sleep every night and didn't care if she was there or not. "I could come in January or February, if you'd like."

"Do whatever you want. It's all the same to me," he said. Whatever human had been in there when her mother was alive had died long since, even before his wife. He was tough on everyone, except Mickie.

"Take care, Dad. I'll call you sometime."

"Say hello to your sister for me when you see her. Send her my love," he added, which hit Billie's heart like a wrecking ball. He never sent his love to her, and didn't have any, except for Mickie, his favorite. There was no room in his burnt-out heart for Billie, and never had been. He cared more about his cows and his dairy than about her. She was too much like her mother, with her nose in her books.

"I'll tell her, Dad. Take care of yourself."

"Yeah, you too," he said, and he hung up. Billie sat

quietly for a minute, recovering from the call. There were tears in her eyes and she wiped them away. The whole story of her miserable childhood was in that call. He had no love to give anyone except Mickie, because she was beautiful and more like him. Billie knew she'd been disqualified at birth. She wasn't a boy and couldn't work on the farm with him. She wasn't strikingly beautiful like Mickie. She was of no use to him whatsoever, and her getting an education had driven them even further apart. She remembered Tom telling her when they were kids that her father was a jerk, and it had been a relief to know that he thought so too. Her mother never admitted it, and always defended him. But at least she defended Billie too. No one else had, except Tom. And he had disappeared out of her life after West Point. It was a huge loss at the time, and still was.

She walked into the living room of the apartment she shared now with Jason. She had offered to pay rent but he had refused and said he didn't need her to, it was a lucky break for her.

He was sitting at the dining table with his laptop and notes all over the place for an article he was writing. He looked up and saw the look on her face. She felt like an orphan, and in a way, she was. Her father had no love for her and never had.

"Well, you can have me for Christmas, if you want me," she said, looking forlorn.

"What happened?" He could see that something had.

"I spoke to my father. He's fine if I don't come home. I think he'd actually prefer it. He hates Christmas, and he loves seeing Mickie, not me. She's the star. I've always been a huge disappointment to him. He thinks I'm a freak. I went to college, which he considers a waste of time. I'm not a boy, and I don't look like her. So I'm useless. It's better this way. I didn't want to go home, it would have been awful. It always is. And it would have been worse without Mickie. I wouldn't have had anyone to talk to for a week. He gets drunk at night." It sounded like a nightmare to Jason, and he was glad she'd been spared. So was she. She looked at him with a wintry smile. "I'm happy I can come with you. It was just depressing talking to him. It puts it all in my face again and reminds me of how bad it was. The only good thing at home for me was my mom, and she's gone. She kind of forced him to pretend he was human when she was alive, but he never was. I realize now how unhappy he must have made her, although he didn't drink as much then. But he's not a nice guy sober either. He never was to me, or to her. He hates education and everything she loved and taught me. My sister has always been more like him."

"Well, I'm going to see to it that you have a fantastic

Christmas," Jason said to her. "We love Christmas at our house. It's going to be great, Billie, you'll see." He pulled her onto his lap and put his arms around her. She fit on his lap like a child, and he wished he could make up to her for the rotten family she got stuck with. It made his heart ache for her, just thinking about it, and he was thrilled she was coming to New York with him. He couldn't wait to tell his parents and for them to meet her.

Chapter 8

The weeks before Christmas were insanely busy for Alex. Every woman he had treated for the last year, even before he moved his practice to Bel Air, wanted some kind of treatment or tune-up before the holidays. Word of mouth, particularly in the Hollywood community, had grown his practice rapidly in the past six months since he had opened his offices in Bel Air and expanded his practice into Bellissima. His new and old patients loved it, and Mickie was a familiar face there now. Her photograph was blown up on his office wall. She circulated among the patients as they left and arrived and chatted with them, and knew many of them.

They thought her an enchanting young woman and enjoyed talking to her. She wore mostly Chanel now, and had bought lots of white pants and white sweaters, and white Chanel jackets to blend into the décor. Sometimes she just wore a white bodysuit, to show off her incredible figure. Alex had instructed her to tell patients she had had either body contouring or cool sculpting if they asked for specifics. And that she'd had both Thermage and regular mesotherapy on her face. She knew just what to say now. Alex was particularly fond of mesotherapy because it was a combination of pharmaceuticals by injection, which allowed him to mix his own blend of secret ingredients and experiment on patients. Most of the time the results were remarkable. There was risk involved because it was not FDA approved, which he glossed over when describing it to patients, and since they trusted him implicitly most of them let him try it. Only the most skeptical or skittish hesitated or decided against it. He was so convincing when he told them about a treatment tailored specifically to them, and seeing Mickie's gorgeous face usually reassured them. It was his favorite treatment, because he could combine so many different elements in the injections. He could add vitamins, use homeopathics, hormones, or enzymes to get different results tailored to each patient. He had a natural talent for his specialty, like an artist. He made women more beautiful.

And just about everyone wanted Botox and bigger lips for Christmas. Some days it felt like an assembly line as he saw as many as fifteen to twenty patients a day, nearly double his usual caseload. He stayed late every night in order to fit them all in before the holidays.

He was doing a delicate collagen thread lift when Wendy came to tell him that he had a registered letter he needed to sign for. There was no way he could leave the procedure to do it. They had hired two more women in the office just to deal with increased billing since June. He had never expected the volume of patients to increase as fast as it had. He had been right to leave Florida and come to L.A. It had taken two years to open his new offices, and the gamble had paid off.

"Can't you sign for me?" he said to Wendy.

"It's registered, no, I can't," she said firmly.

The mail carrier said he would wait. He had to wait forty minutes until Alex finished the procedure, apologized to the patient, and left Wendy with her while he went to sign for the letter. He tossed it on his desk unopened, and came back to chat with the patient until she left, as he always did. Bedside manner was everything in alternate esthetic medicine, as he called it. He refused to call it surgery, since he never used a scalpel.

He had four patients back-to-back after the collagen thread lift, and it was almost eight o'clock that night before he remembered the registered letter on his desk.

Wendy hadn't opened it, since it was registered to his name

and handwritten and she thought it might be personal, so she had left it where he tossed it. He read it in a short stack of other letters. Some were just Christmas wishes, a few were bills for Mickie's clothes. He opened the registered letter last and sat staring at it for a long time. It was from a patient whom he vaguely remembered. He had seen her in July for Botox injections and silicone injections, and never again. Liquid silicone was not approved by the FDA, but he had used it successfully several times. And there was counterfeit Botox on the market, but he was careful about his suppliers.

The woman said that she had spent four months in the hospital due to his treatments and nearly died. He had injected her with liquid silicone without warning her it was not approved. She had had to have surgery to remove it. She was now facially disfigured. The silicone had entered her lungs and nearly killed her. She had had an embolism as a result, and she was filing suit against him civilly, but more important, she had turned her medical files over to an attorney to bring criminal charges against him for attempted murder. The civil suit was frightening enough, but could be settled. Mistakes happened sometimes if a patient had an allergic reaction, and he engaged in delicate procedures. But criminal charges would end his career if he was found guilty. His mesotherapy injections often contained non-FDA approved substances, although some were quite harmless. The liquid silicone was potentially a major problem in a criminal case.

The woman had sent him a handwritten letter so that he would know from her personally, and not just through the courts or the police or lawyers, that he had ruined her life. She had attempted suicide twice since being released from the hospital in November, but had now decided to live at least long enough to see him put behind bars. She had included a photograph of her face and what he saw there made him want to cry, not for what he had done to her, but what it would do to him if the case went to criminal trial. She looked like the Elephant Man. He put it back in the envelope with the letter and put it in a locked drawer in his desk. He hoped that the police would believe she was a crackpot and would drop the case. It was all he could hope for. He didn't dare tell anyone about the letter. He didn't even dare call a lawyer. He was too terrified to think. He just wanted to ignore it and will it away.

He poured himself a stiff drink from the bar in his office, a straight double Scotch, neat. Everyone had gone home by then, and he turned off the lights and went up to the apartment.

Mickie noticed immediately how pale he was, and she could smell the Scotch on his breath when she kissed him.

"Are you okay? You're very pale."

"I'm just tired, long day. Everyone wants something before Christmas." He tried smiling at her but it felt like a rictus, and he felt nauseous and dizzy. He was half terrified the police would show up any minute. His mesotherapy injections were sometimes very creative. He believed in them, but an accident could happen to any doctor, even with a simple procedure if a patient had an adverse reaction.

He went through the motions of sex with Mickie that night but she could barely arouse him. He threw up afterward, and she put him to bed, sure he had the flu.

He was better in the morning, and had sex with her to prove he was, but he felt like a robot all day. He could barely get through the patients he had to see, and was much more cautious than usual with his mesotherapy patients, making their treatments up of mostly vitamins and hormones, and he didn't use liquid silicone all day. He was haunted by the registered letter locked in his desk, not for the patient's sake, but for his own.

It took him four days to stop expecting to see the police at the door. He felt like he could breathe again, and told himself nothing would come of it. And on the fifth day, he got another registered letter. At first he thought it was from the same woman, but it wasn't. It was from another woman who had almost died from a counterfeit Botox injection he had given her, and liquid silicone too. He suddenly realized he must have bought a bad lot months ago, and it was a miracle no one had died. But the second woman was even more severely disfigured than the first one, and she was threatening to hand over her files to the police, and sue him civilly for ten million dollars. She was a flight attendant and could no longer work. She had been in the hospital for months, fighting for her life, and some of the silicone damage had to be surgically removed. The second letter almost did him in. He didn't know what to do. He knew he had to call a lawyer, but no one had brought charges yet, the police hadn't shown up, and there were things in his past he didn't wish to share even with a lawyer, let alone with the press or all the patients in his practice. All he could hope was that the police wouldn't bother to press charges. He was terrified that more women like them would surface. They had waited a long time to hire lawyers and contact him, because they'd been too sick to do so, had been hospitalized, and had wanted to see the extent of the damage after a few months and if it would improve. It hadn't. There were before and after photographs of the second woman, and it was tragic. He sobbed when he looked at them, and locked the second letter up with the first one. He felt like there was a time bomb ticking in the drawer and didn't know what to do with it.

He saw the last of his patients that day and gave his staff their Christmas bonuses. He and Mickie were leaving the next day for St. Barts. He could hardly keep himself together enough to pack, and he threw his clothes into a suitcase that night. Mickie was busy in the guest room she had taken over as a closet, and packing her own clothes in five suitcases, so she didn't see Alex, or notice the shaking hands, the perspiring face, the gray color of his skin, or the terror in his eyes as he packed. He had no idea what he was going to do if the two women went to the police to bring criminal charges against him. He was vulnerable in so many ways.

He called Wendy, his assistant, the next morning before they left, and told her to go to the office and lock up all the brochures, he said he was going to do new ones when he got back. He trusted her and she promised to do it. Alex was well aware that if the police got hold of them, the fraudulent before and after photos of Mickie would be damaging and would not help his case. He did not say that to Wendy. He had replenished his Botox supply since he'd seen those women, and he was certain that his newest supply was not counterfeit. He had used the current supplier before. He promised himself not to use liquid silicone again when he got back. He had gotten lucky too many times, since it wasn't FDA approved. Using it was risky.

They left for the airport with a luggage van driven by one of their security guards. Alex had two valises and Mickie five. She was in high spirits in a beautiful huge straw hat too big to pack, white jeans, a white linen Chanel jacket, and sky blue platform espadrilles. She looked exquisite as they boarded their newly leased jet paid for with the money from the Koreans for the spa in Dallas. And Alex had paid two million dollars to charter the two-hundred-and-eighty-foot yacht, with a crew of twenty-five, to cruise around the Caribbean for two weeks. He intended to use the Korean investors' money to repay the three million dollars he had taken. He could afford to once he went over his accounts for the year, and they didn't need the money for Dallas yet. He and Mickie hadn't invited any guests for New Year's and now he didn't want to. He needed time to think about what he would do if the two women pressed charges. It was all terrifying. He had never had a problem like it before. Everyone loved their treatments and his patients adored him. There were just a few that weren't happy with their results, but that was to be expected, dealing with people's bodies and faces and their sometimes unrealistic expectations. He tried to weed those out but sometimes they slipped below the radar. The two women who had written letters certainly had. But if their photographs were honest and not Photoshopped, they had good reason to be upset, and even to want him behind bars. Their faces were ruined and could never be fully restored.

"You're very quiet," Mickie commented, as they sat across

from each other at the dining table on their new plane. It was beautiful inside and out, and extremely comfortable. It was fitted for twelve passengers and a crew of five: captain, co-pilot, engineer, two flight attendants.

"It's been an exhausting week," he said to Mickie, trying to smile. She walked around the table to bend down next to him and whisper in his ear.

"Don't you think we should christen the plane?" she asked him. There was a luxurious bedroom for them, with a dressing room and bath. Alex looked up at her with a weak smile. "I'll have you shipshape in no time," she whispered to him. "Better than acupuncture," which he firmly believed in for himself when he was stressed or tired. More than that, he was panicked, with a terror that had his guts in a vise-like grip and hadn't let go in six days, since the first letter. He wanted to rewind the film and cut that part out. But he couldn't.

A short time later, Alex thanked the stewardess and followed Mickie to the bedroom, looking very circumspect. It was a nine-and-a-half-hour flight to St. Martin, where the boat was meeting them, and perfectly reasonable that they would take a rest during the flight. Rest was not what Mickie had in mind. She used her most artful tricks that always worked on him, and finally dragged him back from the grim place in his head where he'd been trapped all week. He forgot about everything but Mickie and her magic, as they flew east across the country, heading toward the Caribbean. She tormented him exquisitely for nearly three hours, which emptied his mind completely, and after that he slept for two hours. She lay beside him for a while and then went to read magazines.

Alex emerged from the cabin, looking refreshed five hours later, in time for a lunch of caviar, smoked salmon, and crab salad. The food was superb, and they served his favorite white wine, a Chassagne-Montrachet, while Mickie drank champagne, her drug of choice. She had never gotten into drugs, but she loved alcohol, and had an enormous tolerance for vast quantities of good champagne. They had stocked up on Cristal for her. She had easily become accustomed to the finer things in life in the last six months, thanks to Alex. He wondered how long that would last, if he went to prison. And then he suddenly remembered that a wife could not testify against her husband. He was going to propose to her on the boat, and marry her as soon as they got back to L.A., if she agreed. She was very young, and had said to him right from the beginning that she had no interest in marriage yet. She felt too young to get married, but he had to coerce or bribe her into it somehow. It was crucial that she not be able to tell the truth of what she knew. The before and after photographs alone would make them guilty of fraud. It was all racing through his mind as they headed south into the Caribbean, with the turquoise waters beneath them, and he was already tense again by the time he finished lunch. They went back to their bedroom after lunch to attempt to calm him down again. Mickie could tell that something was bothering him, and she had no idea what. But two weeks on a superyacht would fix anything, and she could take care of the rest.

They landed in St. Martin, and the boat came from St. Barts to pick them up. Alex thanked the crew and said that everything had been flawless, and a luggage van drove to the port to load their luggage on the yacht, appropriately called the *Marry Me,* which made him laugh when he saw it. He'd been more interested in the size of the yacht and the bill than the name when he chartered it. It seemed fortuitous now.

Mickie was stunned when she saw the boat. It looked enormous from the dock. The crew were all lined up on deck in their white uniforms. It looked like part of the royal navy, and she couldn't believe all the features and special comforts that were available, from their own hair salon and spa, fully staffed, to their own movie theater. The master cabin was huge, the most luxurious she could ever have dreamed of, the guest cabins were beautiful, and the sun deck was vast, with a helipad and a swimming pool. Mickie and Alex came back upstairs to drink champagne on deck and watch as the yacht motored out of the port at St. Martin.

They were a gorgeous sight. Mickie had no idea what it had cost and would have been speechless if she knew, but Alex realized this was exactly the vacation he needed, with her, away from all the problems and dangers that were threatening him. Nothing could touch him here for the next two weeks, while they floated away and were waited on hand and foot. It was going to be the best Christmas of Mickie's life. She hadn't even known that boats like this existed, and she couldn't wait to try everything out.

As they motored steadily toward St. Barts, they had sex in the master cabin for the first time, and Alex felt like himself again. And this was only the beginning of the trip. He didn't care how much of the Koreans' money he had spent to charter it, it was worth every penny of the two million dollars, and he would figure out a way to cover it later, if he didn't go to prison first. But he didn't even care about that now. Only two weeks on the motor yacht seemed real.

Billie and Jason's plane landed at JFK with a light snow falling. It looked like a Christmas card, and reminded Billie of Boston. Jason felt invigorated just knowing he was home. He kissed Billie as they landed, and they headed for baggage claim with the other passengers, and then went outside to find a cab. The snow wasn't sticking yet, but it looked pretty as Billie had a frost of it on her hair and eyelashes, and Jason couldn't wait to get to his parents' apartment on Fifth Avenue. It was the same apartment he had grown up in, and the treasures of his boyhood were still in his room. His mother was putting him and Billie in one guest room and his sister and her boyfriend in the other. Their childhood rooms remained as shrines to the past, with all their mementos and souvenirs, trophies and photographs. His sister Emily's blue ribbons from her horse shows, his baseball and basketball trophies. The apartment had a view of Central Park and by the time they got there, the trees were turning white.

"Do you skate?" Jason asked Billie in the cab, and she nodded enthusiastically.

"I love it."

"We'll go tomorrow if we have time," he promised. They chatted animatedly in the cab, both of them excited about what was going to be a wonderful Christmas, better than Billie had ever known, among people who loved each other, were intelligent, and had meaningful jobs. It was the world she belonged in now.

It took them an hour to get to the city. The snow hadn't slowed the traffic down yet. Shoppers and theatergoers and people going to Christmas parties had added to the usual traffic, but the whole city seemed festive to Billie and Jason, coming from L.A. where it didn't look like Christmas at all.

When they got to the building on Fifth Avenue where

Jason's parents lived, the doorman recognized Jason and was happy to see him. A porter helped them get the two bags upstairs. Jason didn't have his key with him and he rang the bell. His parents were waiting for them and his mother opened the door. She was a trim-looking woman in her mid-sixties with attractively dyed brown hair, and was wearing the black suit she had worn to the office. She had rushed home to be there to greet Jason and meet Billie. Jason's father was at home too. He looked very much like Jason and was equally tall, with a thick head of white hair. Jason carried their bags to the bedroom, and Marta, the housekeeper who had worked for them for thirty years, came out of the kitchen to hug him. There were delicious smells emanating from the kitchen, and the table in the dining room was set for four. Jason's sister was arriving the next day from Vermont, so he and Billie would be alone with his parents for the evening.

They looked like people in a movie to Billie. There were warm greetings and hugs, the same housekeeper who had taken care of Emily and Jason when they were children. There was stability and warmth, kindness and comfort evident in every fiber of the tapestry of their lives. They were the kind of family Billie had dreamed of and had never belonged to. She had gone to college with people like Jason at MIT, but she had never been one of them. She had been an outsider wherever she went. She had been considered a freak in Iowa, in a poor farming town where her classmates still married straight out of high school, didn't go to college, and started having babies immediately. Her hunger for learning and books and wanting an education had set her apart from them all her life, even from her own father who had been a stranger to her and treated her like an intruder from another planet. To people like Jason and his parents, she was an outsider too, having grown up poor in a farming town, with a father who ran a dairy farm, and she had none of the sophisticated, educated background they did, traveling around the world and working as doctors and lawyers and publishers. Whichever way she turned, she was out of step. She felt as though she didn't belong anywhere, and was standing out in the cold, looking in through a window. She never belonged with the people she was with.

Billie was quiet as she tried to adjust to her surroundings, and Jason looked at her when they were alone in the pretty guest bedroom with a blue satin bedspread, antique furniture, and flowered chintz curtains in the same blue as the bedspread. He could suddenly sense how out of her element she felt. She had the right credentials to be with them now, but she came from a place that was foreign to his family, and her whole upbringing was shocking by comparison. She couldn't put words to what she was feeling, but Jason could see it in her eyes. She felt like an orphan again. And she was much younger than Jason, which set her apart too. He put his arms around her and held her for a moment.

"Just breathe," he said to her quietly. "I know everything is new, and you don't know anyone here, but they want you to be here, they're happy to meet you. You're safe and welcome here, and I love you. Nothing bad is going to happen. They're not going to send you away. The mean girls are all gone, even your sister, who made you feel like you didn't belong. You belong here because I want you here, and I'm so proud that you came home with me. Take off your coat, and relax." She was still standing in her coat, and he understood how she felt without her having to explain it to him. She hadn't felt that kind of kinship and bond with anyone since she was a kid lying out in a field looking up at the sky with Tom, or by the river with him in the summer. They were the only two people in the world they lived in who spoke the same language. And now she felt the same way with Jason. They were best friends as well as lovers.

She took off her coat, washed her face and hands, brushed her hair, and put on decent shoes instead of running shoes, and they went back to the living room to talk to his parents. She was surprised how easy it was, and how welcoming they were. Jason's father, Robert, was funny and told her stories about Jason getting into mischief as a kid, about the science experiment that had nearly blown up their house in Connecticut, and the time when he and Emily built a tree house and it turned upside down. They were silly stories but they put Billie at ease, and the love among all of them was tangible. It was a living, breathing thing that bound them to each other. She told them how much she had loved Boston and had wanted to stay there, but couldn't find a job, so she wound up in L.A. with her sister, and had met Jason. Robert said his brother had gone to MIT and had become an engineer, and he said it was a great school and he used to visit him there when he was in high school. Robert had gone to Princeton instead because their father had. They were part of the boys' club that had attended MIT and the Ivy League colleges in the old days, and now the student body was more diversified and included people like Billie.

"That's why I went to UCLA," Jason intervened. "I didn't want to go to the schools my family did. I wanted to do something different. I only applied to schools on the West Coast."

The conversation at the dinner table was lively. Robert talked about some of the authors his firm published, and told funny stories about them. Jason's mother, Valerie, talked about a challenging case she was handling, which put ethics in question at the highest corporate level. It was an intelligent exchange among educated people, whose education and interests were similar to hers, and Billie discovered that she did fit in after all. They weren't snobs, they were good people, and by the time she and Jason went to bed in the guest room she felt at home among them, and couldn't wait to meet his sister and her partner. They had talked about Emily's newest book, which was enjoying a modest success, but her parents and Jason thought it was very good and had real merit. His mother gave Billie a copy to read if she wanted to, and she was intrigued, and eager to read it.

When they woke up in the morning, the city was blanketed in snow, and Billie and Jason went for a walk in Central Park after his parents went off to their offices. They went skating as Jason had promised and had fun. And afterward, they had lunch at a famous deli, and took the subway to SoHo and walked around, and then went back uptown. An hour later, Emily and Thad arrived. She was almost as tall as her brother, and had been the captain of the women's basketball team of her high school. Billie felt tiny among them, but comfortable in their midst by then. They had hot chocolate with marshmallows and delicious homemade cookies in the kitchen, just the way they'd had them as kids and still loved them. Billie enjoyed talking to Thad, who had done his residency at Mass General and loved Boston too. He had gone to the University of Vermont, and then got into Harvard Med School.

After dinner, the four young people went to a favorite

bar of Jason's on Third Avenue. They walked through the snow to get there. The atmosphere was festive and fun, and they got back at one in the morning, fast friends by then. Billie was the youngest in the group and they teased her about it.

At the end of the week, they went to the Bells' house in Connecticut, which was rustic and cozy, with a big fireplace in the living room. It was an old colonial farm with small outbuildings around the property. It was the perfect place to spend Christmas.

Billie had brought small gifts for each of them. Jason's mother had given her a white cashmere sweater, which fit her perfectly, and Emily gave her a signed copy of her book, and his father had brought her several books he had published that he thought she would enjoy, including a biography of Marie Curie, which Robert said he had found fascinating.

They went to church together on Christmas Eve. It reminded Billie of her mother. She sat between Jason and Thad at the service, and they sang all the familiar Christmas carols that she loved. When they got back to the house, the two young couples had a snowball fight, and pelted each other with snow, while the parents went inside to light a fire to get warm. Valerie served them hot rum drinks when they came in, covered with snow like little kids, their faces wet and red, their cheeks burning, and laughing as they took their snow-coated coats off, and got warm by the fire. It was a storybook Christmas for Billie. Thad talked about how his parents had gotten divorced when he was young, and were still at war with each other thirty years later, which had made every Christmas difficult. So not everyone had a rosy history like the Bells did. They were well aware of it, and grateful for the family they had, and generous about including others like Thad and Billie.

They spent Christmas Day relaxing and walking in the snow. They cooked a turkey together, and the men were better cooks than the women and teased them mercilessly about it. But everyone made some part of the meal and the results of the joint effort were delicious. They had dinner in the dining room, and it was a warm, congenial meal. Jason's mother, Valerie, watched her son with Billie, and noticed how kind he was with her, and how protective, as though he wanted to shield her from anything that could hurt her. Emily and Thad had a strong, equal partnership. Valerie and Robert watched their children with their partners and were happy to see that they were both with good people who suited them. As far as they knew, Billie was the first girl that Jason had been serious about, or that they had met anyway. She was the first one he had brought home to the family for Christmas, and she was a good addition, helpful, intelligent, fun, and very mature for a girl her age.

She had been through painful things in her youth and had had to grow up quickly. Billie called her father on Christmas morning, he sounded hungover and got off the phone quickly after she wished him a Merry Christmas, and she sent Mickie a text on the boat and she sent back an emoji of Santa Claus.

Emily and Thad left a few days after Christmas. They had to rescue their large dogs from their neighbors. Jason and Billie left on the thirtieth, to spend New Year's Eve in L.A. He had to be back at work the day after New Year's. He wasn't looking forward to it. He and Billie had had such a nice time with his family that they hated to leave and go back to the West Coast. Valerie and Robert hugged Billie and their son when they left, and told her they hoped she would be back soon.

"It's beautiful here in the summer," Valerie said, smiling warmly at her. "Take good care of each other," she said, and both his parents stood in front of the house as they drove away, and as Jason and Billie turned in the car to look at his parents, they saw them kiss and go back inside with Robert's arm around Valerie. It had been a perfect Christmas, and it had been wonderful to see the family that Jason came from, and how close they were. Billie snuggled up next to him in the Uber, and they held hands all the way to the airport to fly back to the world where they lived and worked. It had been a Christmas Billie knew she would never forget, and she would cherish the memory forever.

Chapter 9

Jason had a text from his boss when he reported for work the day after New Year's. He'd had a wonderful vacation with his family, and he had almost hated to come back to L.A. He missed the East at times, particularly New York. It had been fun to be back in the midst of winter and play in the snow. They stayed home on New Year's Eve, watched old movies on TV, and drank champagne Jason had bought. It was perfect, and New Year's Day was balmy in L.A., which wasn't too bad either. The snow was beautiful in Connecticut, but it would be a mess in the city. His parents were going back to work too. The vacation was over. His mother would be going back to her challenging corporate ethics case, and his father had a whole new year of books to publish.

The text Jason had gotten from his boss said to check in with him as soon as he got to work. That usually meant either that he had screwed something up or that they wanted to assign a story to him. He hoped it wasn't another Mafia profile. He was tired of them.

He knocked on his boss's office door at the Crime Bureau. Joe McCarthy was sitting at his desk with a stack of files in front of him, and he looked up as Jason walked in.

"Hi, good holiday?" Joe asked him politely.

"Very nice, thanks. You too?"

"Relatively," Joe said with a grin. He had five young children who were always up to mischief. "One of the kids caught the flu and we all got it. And one of the twins got a broken arm falling out of his new bunk bed. Other than that, it was perfect.

"I have a story for you," he continued. "Investigative. It may just be a few crackpots complaining." The paper got those a lot too. "But where there's smoke, there's fire, some of the time at least. If this is for real, it could be a big story. Stories like this come up sometimes. I'd like you to do some digging and see if you think it's for real.

"I called a couple of my buddies at LAPD, and they say they have nothing on it. I'm not sure I believe them. Either they haven't checked their files, or the women involved haven't called the police, although two of them say they did, or the cops don't know, don't care, or haven't gotten around to it yet." He handed a file across his desk to Jason. "It's medical. We've gotten letters from three women who claim that a local L.A. plastic surgeon injected illegal, non-FDA approved substances into them. All three of them almost died, and if the photos they sent are real, they are seriously disfigured. The pictures are graphic and terrifying. They think the guy is a charlatan."

Joe handed Jason the file. "I looked him up on the internet. Apparently he's a big deal, with an office in Bel Air. He's hot stuff, a society doctor, big with the Hollywood celebrity set, everybody loves him, and he has his own 'beauty center.' He's a plastic surgeon, but doesn't do invasive surgery. But if what these women say about him is true, he's shooting some bad stuff into them, and he's going to kill someone if he hasn't yet, or at least disfigure them, like these three. I don't know if he's careless, a charlatan or a quack, or if these women are crazy. If you find anything out, it's a story worth pursuing, but I'm not looking for a lawsuit if the guy is a reputable doctor. He's a Harvard graduate, so he must know what he's doing. Anyway, you do great research, and this kind of thing is right up your alley."

Jason listened. The story had an uncomfortably familiar ring to it. He hoped that what he was thinking wasn't the case. But it sounded interesting, and Joe was right. If the three women the doctor had disfigured were telling the truth, the doctor needed to be exposed. If they were lunatics, the paper would bury the story. He flipped open the file and got a glimpse of the photographs. They were brutally ugly. The women were completely deformed. There was a before picture of one of them, and the after picture was tragic.

"See what you turn up. Maybe nothing. Or maybe there's a lot more to this story. You never know. I'll tell them to leave you alone on the drug wars and the standard homicides. I'd like you to stay on this until you figure out if there's a story here or not. It could be big, if it's for real." Jason snapped the file shut, and thanked Joe for the assignment. He was smiling. Joe was right. This was the kind of work he loved. He got to play detective and then write about it. You never knew what you'd turn up in the process. This was real journalism, not just a litany of ongoing Mafia killings that had been happening for decades and never seemed to stop. The weapons they used weren't even much different from those they used in Al Capone's day. It was like a time warp except that people were still dying.

"I'll keep you posted on my progress," Jason promised before he left Joe's office, and he went back to his own desk to go through the file carefully. There was one name he hoped he wouldn't find there.

He sat down at his desk, glanced at what he had, and decided to read the letters first so he knew what the claims were. He saw the photographs again and studied them carefully, and then he read the letters from the injured women. Sometimes people went to the press instead of the police, hoping to get media attention or because the police hadn't given credence to the story or didn't care. Or they contacted both in desperation.

The three women were clearly desperate. Their stories were very similar even if the substances varied slightly. Liquid silicone, not FDA approved, which he'd have to check, seemed to be the main culprit, and they said it could have killed them and nearly had. Jason had never heard of counterfeit Botox before but anything was possible. He kept reading and he cringed. There it was. The name he hoped he wouldn't see in the file, and the person who was alleged to be the cause of their tragedies. Alexander Addison IV, Harvard graduate.

Jason sat and stared at the name for a minute, wondering what to do next. Give Joe back the file immediately and recuse himself due to a personal connection? Check it out anyway, and if it came too close to home, then give it back to Joe? Or do the story as if he didn't know anyone involved, and report the truth no matter who got injured in the process? As he closed the file again, he knew what he had to do first, before he did anything else, possibly finding incriminating information that would implicate others. By then, it would be too late. But the name of the doctor didn't surprise him. There was something about what Billie had told him that didn't smell right to him, and he knew it didn't to Billie either. He thought he knew what she would say, but he still had to ask her. He loved her, and he couldn't do this to her with no warning. He couldn't touch the file until he talked to her.

He sent Billie a text. She was at work by then, and he knew how busy she'd be after a holiday. There were people waiting to find out if they had cancer or not. His text said "Please call me as soon as you can." The lack of an affectionate greeting would tell her it was important. She called back in less than five minutes. She was whispering, and calling him from the staff bathroom.

"Hi, what's up? Something wrong?"

"No. Yes. It's about work. Can you meet me for lunch?"

"Did you get a promotion?" she asked, and he smiled.

"Not yet."

"Did you get fired?"

"Not yet either, but I'm working on it," he said, and she laughed. "I need to see you."

"Okay. But I can't stay out too long. Our deli?"

"Perfect. Noon?"

"Great. Bye, I love you." She hung up then.

He was at the deli waiting for her when she walked in wearing her lab coat, her hair in a braid down her back. He looked serious and had a confidential envelope from the paper in his hand. The file was in it.

They sat down at the far end of the restaurant, where it would be quieter. After they placed their order, he got straight to the point.

"I got an assignment from my boss today. It could be a big story or it could be nothing. It's an investigative piece. I have to do the digging myself. To sum it up, three different women want to bring criminal charges against a doctor, a plastic surgeon, for disfigurement, negligence, fraud. They claim he almost killed them. They're permanently disfigured from the substances they say he injected into them, some of them illegal or possibly defective. If it's true, it will be a big story. He could go to prison."

"Who's the doctor?" Billie asked. Her stomach turned over while she waited for the answer.

"You guessed. It's Alex."

"Oh shit," she said, and looked into Jason's eyes.

"I don't give a rat's ass about him," he said honestly, "but depending on what your sister knows, she could go down with him. She may know nothing, even if the charges against him are true. But if she does know, or is involved in some way, even covering up what he does, she could get hurt by this, Billie. Badly. At worst, she could go to prison too. I want to know what you want me to do about it. I can give the story back to Joe now, and tell him I have a personal connection and can't do it. I will absolutely do that if you want me to. If I take the story, I have to follow it to the end, no matter what I find. I don't want to take your sister down with him, but I can't stop the train once I start it. I'm fine if you tell me not to do it. I don't want to start the investigation without your permission," he said simply, as Billie stared at him, her stomach churning. And knowing her sister, she knew anything was possible. Mickie could be in it up to her ears and be fine with it. Or she might know absolutely nothing. Or the three women's claims could be bogus. She was grateful that Jason had given her the option, but ethically, she thought there was only one answer.

"You have to do it," she said simply. "These women deserve a fair shot at the truth."

"If I don't do it, they won't bury it," Jason assured her. "They'll assign it to someone else. That might be the best answer for you, and for Mickie."

"You'll do a better job. She needs to know the truth too, no matter who tells it. If he's hurting people he needs to be stopped, and Mickie needs to get the hell out of there."

"What if she's involved in some way?" Jason didn't think much of Mickie, but felt like an executioner.

Billie took a breath before she answered. "If she's involved, she has to face the consequences. You can't spare her. I don't want her to go to prison, but what you are saying is horrific. Do the story, and I'll just pray she has no part in it. And if she does, she'll have to pay for it."

"Do you want a couple of hours to think about it?" Their lunch came, but neither of them was hungry, and she shook her head.

"No. Do it. It's good for you, and it's better to know the whole story."

"You can't tell her," he said seriously, "or warn her."

"Of course not."

"It's your decision, Billie. I'll give it up in a hot minute if you want me to."

"I don't. For her sake and everyone's, for those women." He nodded, then took the file out of the envelope and handed it to her. It was the last time he could show it to her before he started working on it. She winced and almost cried when she saw the pictures. They were horrendous. "If it's true, the man is a monster."

"He may be. Stranger things have happened. It's not the first time I've heard stories like it," he said.

"Thank you for asking me." She was touched. He didn't

189

even like Mickie, but he loved Billie, and they were sisters. He had done the noble thing, and the right thing. After this, they'd have to see what he would find out, and then what happened when he went to the police with the evidence, which was how it worked.

They both picked at their lunch and finished quickly, so she could go back to work on time, and he could get started. He kissed her when he left her at the hospital door. He was going back to his office to start his research by calling the Medical Board of California to verify that Alex's license was in order. It seemed like a good place to begin.

Jason logged onto the site of the Medical Board of California, clicked on the section for License Verification, put in Alex's name, and waited. Alex Addison's license would be a matter of public record. Jason wanted to know when it had been issued, how long Addison had had a California license to practice. It was an ordinary request and it would be easy to get the information. It seemed to take a very long time and the response came back that there was no medical license issued under that name, which was clearly a computer error. So he called the phone number listed for the Medical Board and made the same request. They left him on hold and came back with the same response. There was no California license issued to a physician by that name.

"He practiced in Florida before. Could he be practicing here with his Florida license?" Jason asked the clerk on the phone, after double-checking the spelling.

"Not legally. It's against the law. Did you check Florida? Maybe he didn't have one there either. Maybe he had a felony on his record, so he couldn't get one. You'd be surprised what people get away with, or try to. You can check Florida, but for a copy of an out-of-state license you have to make the request in writing, and it takes time," the clerk informed Jason, and he thanked him, puzzled that he couldn't find Alex's license. A Harvard-trained physician would not want to practice without a license. Jason wondered if the clerk was right, and Addison had an old felony charge of some kind. He would have to get that information from the police, and he didn't want to contact them yet. That would be further down the road. He was trying to get the simple pieces of the puzzle in place first. Then he'd have to figure out where the pieces of sky belonged, the pieces that didn't fall into place until the very end. He had already hit a wall with a piece that didn't fit, the very first one, and in theory, the easiest one to get. He tried all the standard methods to check for a license in Florida, through the Florida Department of Health and their license verification portal. Nothing showed up. He couldn't find proof of a license in Florida or California.

Jason sat at his desk, thinking about it, and remembered someone he knew in New York. Ed Manning was third-generation Harvard and head of the Harvard Club in New York. He was a lawyer at Jason's father's firm. Jason got the number on the internet and called him. Ed was surprised to hear from Jason. He hadn't seen him in several years.

"I'm writing a piece about a Harvard alum," Jason explained after the initial niceties. "Undergraduate and med school, I need to know what year he graduated. How do I get that info? What department should I call? Is there an alumni office that handles basic inquiries like that?"

"I can get that for you. Give me his name, I'll call you back," Ed said, very obliging and happy to help.

"I hate to put you out," Jason said politely.

"No problem, that's what I do. I'll call you back in a few minutes."

"You're a champ, thanks, Ed."

Jason's cellphone rang ten minutes later.

"No luck, my friend. I checked a couple of different ways. I thought it was a glitch in the system, but it isn't. I checked the registrar's office. We have a bunch of Addisons, but no Alexander. And weirdly, not a single one in the med school. He didn't go to Harvard, undergrad or med. You know, you'd be surprised how many people claim they went to Harvard, and aren't telling the truth. They think no one will ever check. You're smart to fact-check on that. Your Dr. Addison never did."

"You're sure?" Jason pressed him again.

"Absolutely. Nice to talk to you. Give me a call next time you're in New York."

"I will." Jason sat staring into space for a minute. Alex Addison, if that was his real name, which Jason now wondered, was practicing medicine in the state of California without a license. The diplomas that according to Billie's sister hung on his office wall were frauds. He had never gone to Harvard as an undergraduate, or for med school. So where did he go to med school? Or did he? A shudder ran down Jason's spine as he thought of it. Was he even a doctor? It was beginning to get ugly, and he had only just started.

Chapter 10

Coming back from a boat like the *Marry Me,* with a crew of twenty-five, was like being Cinderella after the ball. For two weeks, every crew member had been at Mickie and Alex's beck and call, waiting on them constantly, seeing to their comfort, making their every whim and wish come true. They knew just when to disappear, being an impeccably trained British crew, and the boat had every imaginable comfort and luxury. They were unfailingly discreet, and they would magically appear to provide yet another treat or service and then disappear again until needed. Mickie had never enjoyed anything as much in her life, and Alex had finally relaxed with Mickie's incomparable prowess in bed and ability to satisfy him beyond his wildest imaginings. It was the perfect combination of sex and luxury, lust and fun, excitement and relaxation. By the second week, they wanted to stay forever, and decided not to invite guests, and enjoy it on their own.

Lying on the sundeck one day, with a mojito in her hand and Alex next to her, gently stroking her leg, Mickie said with a sigh, "I want a boat like this." When he glanced at her, he could see that she meant it. She looked dreamy and determined.

"You need a Russian oligarch boyfriend for that, or maybe a Saudi prince, not a plastic surgeon from L.A.," he said, smiling.

"Can we charter it again?" she asked with a sigh.

"I think so . . . I hope so." It had cost him two million, a million a week, because it was the holiday season. Off season it might cost a little less, and he had the Korean money ready to spend to set up the Dallas center. He had dared to spend that much of it for their pleasure because he had other investors in his sights who were sure to come through before he needed the money in Dallas. He had talked to some major investors in L.A., and a young tech genius from Silicon Valley, and he had another Asian group who wanted to meet with him when he got back. He had just gotten a text confirming a meeting with them a few days after he got home. Money had been pouring in for the past few months, and if he made a deal with the

Chinese when he got back to L.A., he would have more than enough money to spend a million for a week on a boat with Mickie. She was getting used to the good life quickly, at an astronomical level, which he wanted to attain too. They had similarly luxurious taste. Alex wanted to start a line of high-priced beauty products, specific to antiaging. It was a lucrative market, particularly in Asia. Products sold for anywhere from six hundred to a thousand dollars per unit, and endorsed by a doctor and properly marketed, he and his investors could make a fortune.

"What does it cost to buy a boat like this?" Mickie asked, curious.

"I don't know. I'm guessing maybe fifty million. You have to have a hell of a lot to spend that kind of money, and maintain it. Boats are money pits," he said. Several of his patients had yachts, and had invited him on them for a day or a weekend. Most of them kept their boats in the Caribbean in the winter and the Mediterranean in the summer. It was a lifestyle he and Mickie both enjoyed and would have no trouble getting used to. Meals that were perfection, swimming in the sea, having sex in a secluded corner of the deck under the stars at night, a never-ending river of champagne, massages whenever they wanted them, a crew dedicated to their every whim. It was easy to see why Mickie loved it, and so did he. The art alone on the boat was worth more than the boat itself.

"It's a long way from Iowa," she said, smiling at him, and he laughed.

"I grew up in a wealthy family," he said, "but it's a long way from Palm Beach for me too. It gives us something to aspire to," he said. He told her about the meeting with the Chinese then, and she looked puzzled.

"Why do you need more investors?" she asked him.

"So I can buy you a boat like this one day," he quipped, and then looked serious. "You can never have too many investors, or too much money. I want to start a line of high-end medically approved antiaging beauty products. There is huge money in that market. The group we're meeting with from Hong Kong is worth billions. They're heavily invested in luxury brands and lifestyle. The Koreans were just the beginning. Beauty is a big market there. The Hong Kong boys are broader scope and more global. My little center in Bel Air is peanuts to them." He had reached out to the Hong Kong investors himself and they said they were interested. "You can't tell anyone about any of this, Mickie. No one. Not even your sister. Especially about our Asian friends. The Korean group has very diverse investments and they don't like anyone knowing their business. We don't want to upset them. They can be very tough to deal with. The Hong Kong group is more refined, but you never know what rivalries exist between them."

"I don't tell Billie anything. She doesn't get it. She doesn't understand anything at this level. She couldn't even imagine it. She's happy with her little job and her little life and her snotty boyfriend. He doesn't 'approve' of me. You can smell it. He's such an asshole."

"You don't need them in your life, forget them," Alex said dismissively. "They're inconsequential people. You have me now, and all this." He waved grandly around him and Mickie agreed. She didn't miss her father, or her mother, and if it came to that, she knew she wouldn't miss Billie either. It had just been convenient to have her come out so she could keep the apartment. But she didn't need her anymore, with Alex in her life.

Alex had intended to ask Mickie to marry him while they were on the boat. He would have done it if he thought he was at serious risk of a court case, but by the second week on the boat, he had regained his perspective and the two women in L.A. threatening to bring charges against him seemed very far away now, and very small in the scheme of things, at the level on which he was operating. If they got too strident, he would settle with them. That would keep them quiet forever, and he could afford to buy them off with the investment money he was pulling in. No one was going to listen to their pathetic claims, and they couldn't prove anything. It wasn't his fault if they'd had a bad reaction. Things happened in the practice of medicine that you couldn't always predict. And marrying Mickie seemed like too big a response to a situation that might never be a problem. Lying in the sun, being waited on, floating on a superyacht in turquoise water with a drink in his hand and a gorgeous twenty-year-old girl perched on top of him made the two complaining women shrink to nothing in his mind. It didn't warrant a hasty marriage, which would cause other legal problems. Marriage had never been a goal for him, and he knew it wasn't for Mickie either. He was willing to be generous with her, but not give her half of everything he had, and people challenged prenups and sometimes won, or got big settlements. Alex didn't want to take the risk, and decided against a proposal, which seemed unnecessary to him. He was no longer panicking, and he stopped thinking about the two women halfway through the trip. Money was power and he had a lot of it now, and he was well on his way to more, and nothing was going to stop him and slow him down.

When they finally left the boat, reluctantly and with regret, having their own plane to take them home made the reentry process a little less painful. They weren't sitting on their suitcases on the dock, they were flying home in the utmost comfort, to see the Hong Kong group a few days later. Mickie was all prepped to look spectacular and not say anything during the meeting or to anyone after. Alex was using her as window dressing, and proof of his talent, and nothing more. She was like a billboard by the side of the road.

One of their security guards picked them up at the airport with the Bentley. When they got home, Mickie unpacked as Alex went down to the office to check his mail. He was feeling relaxed and healthy, after swimming in the sea every day, and exploring beaches with sugar-fine sand.

When he got to his desk, he saw another registered letter. The head security guard had signed for it and placed it on his desk. The first two letters had panicked him, the third one didn't. He glanced through it, and it was more of the same. The woman claimed to have been permanently disfigured by liquid silicone injections. It had gone to her lungs and she'd nearly died. Alex was blasé as he read it. Who would believe her? She was some little housewife in Pasadena whom no one knew. He never had patients sign releases because he didn't want them knowing what was in the injections. It was his own personal magic, and the less they knew the better. He put the letter in the locked drawer with the others, and he went back upstairs to Mickie, lying on the bed in a pale pink transparent negligee watching TV. She asked him what he wanted her to order for dinner.

"You," he said simply, took his clothes off, dropped them on the floor, and joined her on the bed, much to his delight minutes later.

Later that night, on the day Jason told Billie about the accusations against Alex Addison, he brought her up-to-date over dinner in the kitchen, since the investigation hadn't started in earnest yet. He considered it part of the initial warning.

He made pasta and a salad, and looked somber as he told her what he had discovered.

"I found out that he doesn't have a California license to practice medicine, which is stupid of him. It's probably just laziness, and he thought he'd get away with it, since he has such important clients. Or it could be negligence, but that seems unlikely. I'm sure he knows he needs a California license to practice medicine legally in the state.

"The second thing I found out today proves him to be a liar, which is more disturbing. He never went to Harvard, undergrad or medical school. I called a reliable source and he checked the alum records. Addison probably went to some unknown medical school somewhere, which wouldn't impress anyone, so he got two fake Harvard diplomas and stuck them on the wall. He could probably be charged with fraud for that. Together, no license to practice in California and the fake diplomas doesn't make him look good, especially in light of the gravity of the accusations. Three women's lives are ruined because of him. And the authorities can't even pull his license since he doesn't have one. I'm sure he'll have some lame excuse, but the few facts we have don't play in his favor."

"What are you going to do now?" Billie asked him, and he looked pensive.

"I'm not sure. If we hit too many roadblocks, we'll have to turn it over to the police sooner than I thought. They have much better access than I do, and the guy at the records bureau had a point. If Addison has a felony on his record somewhere, unrelated to his practice, or medicine at all, he would lose his license, so that could be why he has no license. The Harvard thing is really disturbing, because he flat-out lied. I have to figure out what to do next. I need to talk to my boss, and let him figure out when we reach out to the police and ask for their help. I wrote to the Bureau of Records in Florida, to see if he had a license there, but it could take weeks, or months, to get an official answer if they're slammed, and I tried to find it online, and couldn't find a record of his license from when he practiced there. The cops can get it a lot faster." It was an upsetting situation, and Billie worried about her sister all night.

A fourth letter arrived on Joe McCarthy's desk that week, similar to the first three, which told both Joe and Jason that they were right to be investigating Addison, and another letter came by the end of the week. It was no longer a case of looking for the source of the smoke, it was turning into a good-sized fire, and heading toward an alarming blaze. Jason told Joe about Addison's lack of a California license, and what he'd heard from Harvard. Added all together, there was no way to turn back now. They had to press forward and get to the bottom of this.

Jason told Billie about the additional letters. There were five irreparably damaged women now, all injured around the same time, which supported the theory that Addison had unwittingly bought a batch of counterfeit Botox, and in addition was using illegal liquid silicone. It was odd that none of his important clients were complaining, and Jason wondered if Alex was aware that he'd gotten a bad lot of the counterfeit substance and used it on less important clients, and only used the good stuff on the highly visible patients with celebrity status, but that idea was so cynical that even he didn't believe it. It seemed more likely that the use of the counterfeit drugs had been accidental and had caused a sudden explosion of tragic injuries, for which Alex was responsible and would have to face the consequences.

And knowing what she knew now, Billie was sick with worry for her sister, and had nightmares every night.

Alex had gotten the fourth and fifth letters too, and added them to the three in the locked drawer in his office. He still didn't know what to do about them, but the police hadn't shown up, and the media hadn't contacted him. He was still hoping that the damaged women would disappear into thin air. Approaching them with a settlement offer was much too dangerous and would be an admission of guilt. They could ask for a fortune, which would wipe out every penny he had from investors, including the Koreans. He couldn't risk it. He just had to lie low and hope to hell they disappeared, and didn't go to the press or the police. It added a constant layer of tension to his life. He tried to pretend it wasn't happening while treating his patients, and Mickie and her own special brand of magic was the only thing keeping him sane.

As he had with the Koreans, Alex orchestrated the dinner with the investors from Hong Kong to perfection. Perfect menu, perfect wine, perfect setting at the Chateau Marmont. They were more international and polished than the Koreans had been. The Koreans had been a little less sophisticated than he'd expected, although very smart in business. The Hong Kong investors had been introduced to him by a big money man in L.A. whom Alex respected. They were elite and high-end, brilliant with their invest-ments, and very interested in the beauty industry. If they came through for him, he would be rolling in money shortly. Making sure the evening went well distracted him totally from the letters in the locked drawer in his office, although he was concerned that he must have bought a bad batch of Botox, some counterfeit, without knowing it, and was grateful that none of his important clients had suffered the same effects.

He had told Mickie what to wear. He wanted her in dressy black Chanel. More class, less sex, and lots of elegance and charm. She was a chameleon and could adapt to every situation, and had so far.

"If we play our cards right, I can take you on another boat trip," he teased her while they were getting dressed, and she emerged from her dressing room in a dress he hadn't seen before, a subtly sexy ladylike black Chanel dress that was strikingly chic. She had done her hair in a loose bun. She looked young but very grown-up, and she looked fabu-lous in the dress. She was sensational in everything she wore. And she had the perfect instinct not to say too much.

They arrived early at the private room at the Chateau Marmont to check everything out. Alex had ordered flowers, which decorated the elegant private dining room, and there was a terrace for their use. There were four men this time, all dressed elegantly in Hermès ties and impeccably tailored suits from the best tailor in Hong Kong, and they were beautifully groomed, spoke perfect English, and included Mickie in the conversation, which the Koreans hadn't. As the evening progressed, it became clear that they wanted to invest in Alex's future antiaging product business, which would require technical research, but they also wanted his consultation to set up an enormous beauty center in Hong Kong, where his formulas would be used. There would even be a five-star hotel where people could stay while they were getting treatments. The investors wanted it to be a complete beauty experience combining Western and Asian techniques, with Alex designing it all.

The head man glanced at Mickie several times and addressed his comments to her as well. They had a very clear vision of what they wanted, which would be a lot for Alex to deliver. It was a huge operation compared to the personal, individualized, small-scale style of Bellissima, and the men were willing to invest twenty-five to thirty million dollars in the project, possibly more. Alex was nearly dizzy with the scope of their plans and the money he could make.

The Hong Kong investors wanted to fund a large-scale operation, and expected it to make a fortune. Alex would have to regularize his treatments so that they were less individually designed, and others would have to be trained to administer them. It required some thought as to how he could pull it off. They wanted to know if Mickie would be interested in spending time in Hong Kong as well. Alex gave her a quelling look, willing her not to give them a definite answer, until he had time to figure out how to do it. Perfectly on cue, she charmed them without committing to anything definite.

Alex promised to give their proposal a great deal of thought, to see how he could take on such a large project without losing the individualized treatments he was famous for. He explained to them that no two treatment plans were the same, just as no two women were the same. They suggested computerized programming, and communication where he could be present at every consultation by Zoom, at least at the outset until he felt confident that the staff could handle it without him when he wasn't there. It was an interesting concept and a leap into big business. Alex wanted to make big money, even billions eventually, and these investors were the right people to make it happen. He had read about them online, and their reputation was pure gold.

The evening ended on a strong positive note, and Mickie looked at Alex in awe on the way home. He had driven them there himself in the Aston Martin. As they left, one of the Hong Kong men had smiled when he saw the car and said he had the same model, and they had talked cars for a few minutes.

"Wow," Mickie said as they drove away. The Hong Kong investors had come to the meeting in a chauffeured Rolls. They weren't afraid to show their wealth. "That sounds like some project. Do you think you could do it?" It was so much bigger than what they were doing in Bel Air, which had a warm personal touch on a tiny scale compared to what the Hong Kong investors envisioned.

"I'd sure as hell like to try," he said, as awestruck as she was. "It's a big leap from where we are right now. Two or three years from now I know I could, at the rate we're growing, but they're anxious to get started. How do you feel about spending time in Hong Kong with me?" he asked her. She was an essential part of his life now, in every way. He had never intended to become dependent on her, personally or professionally, but she was so adaptable, and good at what she did, that he realized he was relying on her, far more than he ever wanted to be or thought could happen. She was a clever girl, more than he had ever suspected in the beginning when he thought she was just a pretty face and a great body. She had a brain that moved as fast as his own, and at times was even more devious. The Chinese investors were aware of the importance of her presence too, and at the end of the evening, had given her their business cards, just as they did to Alex. They would have been stunned if they knew she was twenty years old.

"I'd love to go to Hong Kong," she answered him. She was afraid of nothing. There was no risk she wouldn't take, but she was also smart and looked out for herself. She had never been out of the country, except on the boat to St. Bart's, and she loved the idea of spending time in Asia.

"We'd almost have to commute for a while," he said pensively. He was trying to make the mental leap from Bellissima to what the Hong Kong investors had proposed.

"Can you do that and keep your patients happy here? And what about the center in Dallas? That's quite a stretch," Mickie commented.

"I have to figure it out." The Hong Kong investors wanted to speak to him again in a week or so when he had given their proposal some thought.

He was in high spirits when he got back to the house, and Mickie was excited too. She had been fascinated by their vision and everything they said. Alex had a lot of figuring to do.

Mickie was taking off her dress in her dressing room, when she got a text from Billie.

"I need to talk to you. When can I see you?" It sounded urgent, and Mickie was annoyed. She didn't have time to spend with her sister. She had more important things to do. She texted back "Why?" and Billie responded, "It's important." And then followed up with, "Alone and not at your house." Mickie had no intention of inviting Billie to the house. She looked like a student on a road trip. She didn't fit with Mickie's new image. Mickie was living at a higher level now, and Billie didn't fit into that picture.

"The bar at the Bel Air Hotel, six P.M. tomorrow. Okay for you?" Mickie answered her. It was near the house and she didn't have to go far.

"See you then. Thanks. Love you, B." Mickie hoped she didn't have a problem and wasn't asking for money. That wasn't usually her sister's style, but it sounded urgent. She had no intention of sharing the windfall that might be coming her way as part of Alex's project in Hong Kong, or even the check that he had given her not to return to Stanford, a treat Billie knew nothing about. Mickie was having a bikini wax at seven and she didn't intend to stay with Billie for long.

Billie wanted to talk to Mickie just once, to try to warn her that there was a storm ahead, without violating Jason's confidence. She wasn't sure what she'd say, but she wanted to warn her sister to get out while she could. Mickie had no idea what was coming. From her perspective, things were just getting good, and she had no intention of going anywhere. She wanted to cash in when Alex did. The good times were coming. She had waited all her life for this. And so had Alex.

Chapter 11

Mickie drove to the Bel Air Hotel the next day in the Bentley. Alex didn't let her drive the Aston Martin, and she didn't want to. She didn't bother to take a security guard with her. She didn't feel in any danger. She thought Alex was paranoid about that and it made him feel important to have security guards outside the house. They were provided by a service that rotated them. They all looked to Mickie like actors pretending to be bodyguards. It was a short drive from Bellissima to the Bel Air Hotel.

Billie took an Uber from the hospital when she finished work. She still didn't have a car, and Jason used his Jeep most of the time, but he let her borrow it when she was desperate for a car, which wasn't often.

When Billie got to the hotel, she was wearing her work

clothes, which that day were running shoes, a pink sweater, and jeans. She looked clean and respectable but she still dressed like a schoolgirl. She didn't need fancy clothes to work in the lab. She waited in the garden for Mickie to arrive, watching the swans glide around and trying to figure out what to say to her without saying too much. She didn't want to break her promise to Jason, but she wanted to give Mickie some kind of warning that the roof might fall in, and she didn't want her to take a fall for Alex, if he was doing something illegal, and somehow implicated her. Billie didn't trust him. And her instincts were still to protect her baby sister. Old habits died hard.

Mickie showed up on time in a silver Chanel jogging suit with matching running shoes and a silver Chanel purse. Her clothes no longer appeared secondhand. They were all the latest styles, and Alex was paying full price for them.

Mickie didn't look happy to see her, and Billie was worried and tense. They went to the bar together, Mickie ordered champagne by the glass and Billie water. She wanted to be as coherent as possible to choose her words. She was walking a thin line between concern for her sister and respect for Jason.

"I'm sorry to drag you here on short notice," Billie said for openers.

"So what's the problem?" Mickie didn't want to waste

time with her. She had none of Billie's protective instincts except for herself.

"I don't know what to say or quite how to say it, but I'm worried about you with Alex," Billie got right to the point. It was clear that Mickie didn't want to make chitchat, and neither did she. It was a storm warning, not a social visit. And Mickie considered herself much too important to spend time with Billie now. She had outgrown her.

"Oh, for chrissake, Billie. I've been with him for seven months, and nothing bad has happened. All that crap you were afraid of in the beginning was completely off base. The guy is a serious doctor, he has a practice of every rich, important, or famous woman in L.A., and some men, he makes a shitload of money, and I don't know what you're worried about. I think you're just jealous because I fell into the pot of gold at the end of the rainbow and you can't stand it. You've always been jealous of me, since we were kids."

Billie wanted to scream listening to her, but stayed calm. "I'm not jealous of you. We want different things in life. You have a right to the things you want. And I'm happy for you if it's working for you. I can't tell you how, but I've heard some things that suggest Alex may not be everything he says he is. He could wind up in trouble, and I don't want you in trouble along with him."

Mickie laughed out loud. "We had dinner last night with people who want to invest twenty-five or even up to forty million dollars in his business. I'd call that pretty darn successful. What the fuck are you talking about?"

"I can't tell you, but for instance, he may not have gone to Harvard. It's just a rumor I heard."

"So where did he go? Yale? He's a brilliant doctor, he's more educated than you are. You think you're such hot shit because you went to MIT. So fucking what, where did it get you? You're a lab tech at Cedars." She wanted to hurt Billie, but her sister refused to take the bait.

"I'm only here because if he ever gets in trouble, I don't want you to get hurt with him. That's my only motive here. I'm not trying to spoil your fun. I'm trying to protect you."

"I don't need your protection. This is all about that asshole you live with, isn't it? He hates me, and I don't like him either. He doesn't approve of me, and I don't care. You're picking on one of the most successful doctors in L.A. He has a fantastic practice, and I have a great life with him. What do you want me to do? Walk out on him because of some witch hunt your jerk of a boyfriend is on? Do you want me to live in a shit apartment like the one I shared with you? I am living the life I always wanted, and I don't give a damn how jealous you are of me, I'm not giving that up and going back to being a waitress because you think it's all I deserve because I didn't finish high school. Fuck you, Billie, and your boyfriend." She stood up then, reached into her silver Chanel bag, pulled out a twenty-dollar bill, and dropped it on the bar to pay for her champagne. "I don't need you in my life. I don't want you in my life. Just stay away from me. I don't know who you've been talking to, but it's all bullshit. Yeah, I have a fantastic life now, so get over it. This is all about how jealous you are of me, you're consumed by it. It goes all the way back to Dad because he liked me better than he liked you. Well, I'm sorry, that's not my fault." All the venom of her twenty years was spewing out on her sister. She was so blind to Alex's faults that the possibility that he might not be what he claimed was inconceivable to her. And her jealousy and resentment of Billie knew no bounds. It was a painful eye-opener for Billie, and a reminder of the past and her earlier experiences with her sister. But she had at least tried to warn her. Her conscience was clear. It was useless and Billie couldn't tell her about the five women whose faces were deformed because of Alex. "Just stay away from me," Mickie repeated. "Stay out of my life," she said, and walked out of the bar, went to claim her car from the valet, got in, and drove away.

Billie took a sip of her water and left Billie's money on the bar, added a little more for the tip, and then she got up and left too. She called an Uber once she left the bar, and it arrived three minutes later. She was silent on the drive back to West Hollywood, thinking about everything Mickie had said. Billie just hoped that Alex didn't drag her down with him, but he might. There was nothing she could do about it. She went upstairs to the apartment, and sat thinking about Mickie. She really was a lost cause. Billie felt like she didn't even have a sister. Mickie really didn't care about anyone but herself.

While Billie was meeting with her sister, Jason was in Joe McCarthy's office discussing their next steps. They had the five women's letters on the desk between them, all with photographs.

"He's practicing without a license, and he didn't go to the school he claims. The truth is we don't know a damn thing about him, and the police have better access than we do. They can at least give us some history from Florida, and check for a criminal record nationally. We don't know where he went to medical school, or even if he did," Jason said, going to the most extreme possibility, which he doubted was the case. "I assume he's a doctor, but why no license? No one is that sloppy. And he's never had a problem until these five women, but their evidence is irrefutable. We need to know a lot more about this guy. I think we need to give it to the police now." They would have to eventually anyway to pick up any criminal activity, but they needed more help from them now, since nothing was adding up so far. "I just want your green light to go to them now. I didn't want to do it without talking to you."

"I agree," Joe said with a serious expression. "We need their database, their muscle, and their connections."

"Do you want to call them or should I?" Jason asked him.

"You can call them. It's your story. I know the head of the fraud unit, Lieutenant Dan Kelly. I'll send him a text and give him a heads-up. You have my blessing on this." Joe glanced at his watch. It was five-thirty. "I'll shoot him a text now. Call him in five minutes, and see if he wants you to send him what you've got, or meet with him on Monday." Joe jotted Kelly's phone number down on a piece of paper and handed it to him, and Jason went back to his desk. He waited five minutes, and called the number Joe had given him. A gruff voice answered.

"Kelly," he said in a voice that sounded like he had the weight of the world on his shoulders.

Jason gave him a quick rundown of what he had so far, and the lieutenant listened carefully before he spoke.

"We've had cases like this before, probably not at this level. You wouldn't believe the people who practice without the benefit of medical school, let alone a license. That's probably not the case with this guy, with such a successful high-end practice. It sounds like he may have bought a load of counterfeit products and didn't know it, and now they're coming back to haunt him. The silicone issue is another story, if it's not cleared by the FDA. If he didn't have the women sign a release, I hope he's got great malpractice insurance. The fake diplomas are fraud, of course. I'd like to get a background on him so we know what we're dealing with. Some people just think they're above the law. And I wonder if he got himself in trouble of some kind in Florida. Send me the file digitally, and I'll get the ball rolling from here. We probably won't get much over the weekend. I'll let you know if we do. Otherwise, I'll call you when we've got something. Let's find out what Dr. Alexander Addison the Fourth has been up to," he said, and Jason liked the sound of him. Dan Kelly was taking the matter seriously, and he hadn't even seen the horrifying photographs of the women yet. He didn't know if his victims had sent their letters and photographs to the police, as they had threatened to do.

Jason left his office at six and got home minutes after Billie returned from her meeting with her sister. She looked shaken and he could see that something was wrong.

"Hard day at work?" he asked her. She took it to heart sometimes when they had bad news for the doctors to deliver to their patients. There was a story behind each one, and a real live human being.

"I just had a drink with Mickie," she said quietly.

"Oh? How was that?"

"I didn't give away any secrets. I just said that I'd been hearing things about Alex and I'm concerned. She went nuts and accused me of being jealous of her. She said someone is considering investing twenty-five million dollars in his practice. She told me to stay out of her life. She hasn't changed a bit. Same old Mickie. I don't know why I thought it would be different with her this time. She's vicious when you get in her way. She doesn't want anything interfering with her life with Alex."

"I think you ought to steer clear for a while. Things could get messy," Jason said carefully. "We turned the investigation over to the police today. We need their help. It's in the hands of the fraud unit now. They'll do a national search on Addison. They're very efficient." He was sorry that Billie's sister had beaten her up, although it didn't surprise him. There was something about her that affected him viscerally. Mickie was young, but he had the sense that she was a bad person, somewhere deep inside her, there was something evil lurking. Billie was so innocent she didn't see it, or maybe she did but didn't want to believe it.

They made dinner and streamed a movie and went to bed early, and had a quiet weekend. Jason wondered how soon the police would get back to him and Joe, and what they'd come up with. His instincts told him that there was a lot more to Alexander Addison than they knew so far.

Mickie and Alex spent the weekend talking about their dinner with the investors from Hong Kong, and how to make their concept work. The scale was so large that Alex couldn't see how to do it yet, but he wanted their money. Mickie was more enthusiastic about Hong Kong than he was, but he was determined to find a way. They drove to Santa Barbara on Saturday and spent a night at the Biltmore. On Sunday, they went to the pool at the Coral Casino, and came back to L.A. that night. They'd been talking about the Chinese investors all weekend.

Mickie paid no attention to what her sister had told her when they met at the Bel Air Hotel on Friday. She didn't care what she thought. Alex was a brilliant doctor, and he had a booming business, and a fantastic future ahead of him. He took good care of her, and she was convinced that Billie was jealous. Mickie didn't need Billie anymore. She wasn't fourteen years old now. She didn't need her help. She could fend for herself. She had exactly the life she wanted with Alex, and she wasn't going to let anyone interfere with that, least of all her pathetic sister and her pompous, judgmental boyfriend. They meant nothing to her. Alex was the main event in her life now. The only event. And if he could figure out how to do it, he had twenty-five million dollars coming his way from Hong Kong, and maybe more. Mickie planned to be right there with him when he got it. She wasn't going to let Billie change that or rob her of the opportunity by lying about Alex. She didn't even care if some of the rumors were true about him. He was making a fortune, with a bigger one in his future. That was all she cared about.

On Monday, life went back to normal. Alex saw patients and Mickie went shopping. Billie went to work and tried not to think about her sister and the things she had said. Jason had an article to write. Alex was obsessing about Hong Kong, and he had put the five ugly letters in his locked desk out of his mind. He had convinced himself that the women who had written them weren't going to do anything about it. Nothing could stop him from the success he deserved. They were nobodies and didn't matter, as far as he was concerned. And those women were no great beauties to start with, in his opinion. They had no right to impede his progress.

On Tuesday morning, Lt. Dan Kelly sent Jason a text and asked him if he was free to come and see him at eleven. Jason said he'd be there, and Kelly sent him the codes to get into the building.

He arrived on time, in the midst of the chaos of the fraud unit, and was led to the lieutenant's office by a female detective. Kelly stood to greet him. He was a big man, and he thanked Jason for coming.

"Of course. I take it you have some news of the doctor," Jason said. There was a long printout on Kelly's desk amid stacks of papers and files, and Dan Kelly looked serious as he waved Jason to the chair across from him.

"Miami helped us out a lot. And NYPD gave us some background too. This guy's got a long history. There's going to be a lot of media attention on this." He picked up the printout so he could go over it chronologically. "He started out as Angelo Alvarez, in Hell's Kitchen in New York. Cuban father who drove a garbage truck for the city. He was killed in an accident when Angelo was thirteen, and the mother had disappeared at some point before that. Angelo wound up in foster care when the father was killed. He had trouble with his placements, stealing from his foster families and in school. He wound up in juvenile hall, in and out of trouble after that, mostly petty theft and causing trouble at juvie, but apparently a bright kid, emancipated at sixteen, never finished high school. He was living on the Lower East Side, delivering food for a Chinese restaurant, got busted for possession, was sent back to juvie, and moved to Miami when he got out. He was about eighteen. I don't know where he got the money, maybe selling drugs, but he went to beauty school in Miami when he was eighteen or nineteen, and spent ten years as a hairdresser in Miami. He got busted for selling drugs to his clients, was sentenced to a year in jail, served about six months, and went back to hairdressing. He went to work for some high-end spa where he did hair, and apparently got into beauty and facials, and my guess would be that somewhere around then he started messing with more than facials, maybe Botox shots. He changed his name to Alexander Addison the Fourth, and moved to Palm Beach and worked for a spa there. He switched from hair to skincare. He moved to L.A. about four years ago, and that's when he became Dr. Addison, and apparently he was giving medical beauty treatments for three years in a house in Beverly Hills. He picked up some wealthy clients, who gave him financial backing, quite a lot of it in fact, and he got enough money together to open the place he's running now that he calls Bellissima, which he opened seven months ago, in June. He's been practicing medicine without a license for at least four years that we know of, and making a hell of a lot of money at it. No one's ever brought complaints against him until these five women, so something must have gone wrong. He has eleven million dollars in the bank, ten of which came from Korea in November. His bank is working with us to investigate the source. We've had some other scams come out of there, and my guess and the bank's is that his investors there are laundering money by investing in legitimate businesses in the States. They probably didn't know that he's running a fraudulent business himself, practicing medicine without a license and no training. He's spending a hell of a lot of money these days. He just spent two million over Christmas to charter a yacht in the Caribbean, and he just leased a jet for another million. My second guess is that he's using the Koreans' money for that and they don't know it. It's probably the slickest operation I've seen for a guy practicing medicine with no medical training whatsoever. Sometimes you get nurses doing that, or guys who served as paramedics in the military. The only training he's had is as a hairdresser twenty-five years ago, and he didn't go to school past tenth grade. Between the fancy name, his good looks, the pretense that he went to Harvard, he's been pulling it off on a major scale for at least five years, and maybe longer in Palm Beach. He managed to get at least ten million dollars out of investors in Korea recently and maybe five out of other investors in L.A. You've got to hand it to him. Now he has seriously damaged five women's faces and nearly killed them. But until now, he's gotten away with it. The guy must be a genius."

"Or a brilliant sociopath," Jason said, stunned by the information the lieutenant had shared with him. "What happens now?"

"It's a complicated process," Kelly responded. "First we get a warrant for his arrest, so we stop him from harming anyone else. The charges will be mostly fraud and practicing medicine without a license, great bodily harm of the five women who contacted you, and criminal negligence. We'll check out the money laundering aspect. We'll shut down his operation and seize everything in the house, and all the medical substances in his office will go to our lab for testing to see what he's been shooting into his 'patients.' They're all felony charges. If he pleads guilty, we'll see where it goes, but he'll serve time, mostly because of the five women. And once it goes public in the press, other victims may come forward. If he doesn't plead guilty, we go to trial, and the D.A. will have a field day. Any way you look at it, Mr. Addison is going to serve a lot of time. You hit the jackpot on this one."

"What about his employees? Will they be charged too?"

"As a rule, no. Guys like this don't share their secrets. They play it very close to the vest. If his employees were knowing accomplices, then yes, they'll be charged too."

"Apparently every supply closet has a combination lock, and only he knows the combination," Jason told him.

"That makes sense, if he's using drugs he shouldn't, that aren't federally approved, or not for human use, which happens too. Usually these guys hire real nurses, who may or may not have suspected that what he was doing wasn't legal. He has half a dozen employees. I think several of them are nurses. He has a girlfriend. We'll talk to her, but she probably doesn't know anything. She's probably just window dressing." Jason stopped him then and held up a hand.

"Just for full disclosure here. I live with the sister of his girlfriend. I don't think she has the remotest idea he's not a doctor. She's twenty years old, and she was hired as a model for his ads. If you'd like me to stay out of the investigation, I will. I'm not close to her."

"You've already proven yourself here. Does your partner know anything about him, that you're aware of?"

"Her sister doesn't tell her anything and has total faith in the guy. My partner and I have had bad feelings about him, but we never knew anything, it was just a feeling. He seems to be pretty arrogant."

"He got away with it for a long time. Some of these guys get away with it for twenty years, and then someone dies, the whole thing gets exposed, and all hell breaks loose. That will probably happen here when his fancy celebrity clients read about him. They're all going to be panicked over whatever he was doing to them. This won't go quietly into the night. He has too many important patients, and his patients and investors are going to be pissed. I don't imagine his Korean friends will be too happy either. Any money he has now, or property, may be distributed among the victims, so the Koreans will lose their ten million, if he hasn't already spent it by then anyway."

"He's currently negotiating with some investors, but I don't think there's been any conclusion of that deal." Jason supplied what Billie had told him.

"Ambitious guy," Kelly commented. "If he'd kept it small and below the radar, he might never have gotten caught. You've saved lives by shining a spotlight on it. It's going to take time to interrogate as many people as we can, patients, his employees, his girlfriend, his medical suppliers. If it goes to trial, there will be a lot of testimony, from a lot of important people and celebrities. It will be a media circus, you can be sure of that."

Listening to the lieutenant, Jason almost felt sorry for Mickie. She was about to get caught in a maelstrom of accusations and the interrogations to find out what she knew would be intense. It was going to be a lot to go through. Jason couldn't help wondering if they would keep her clothes to sell for the benefit of the victims. It was a possibility, since Alex paid for them. But as much as he disliked her, Jason suspected that she was innocent, and had been as duped as everyone else, but at least she'd had fun in the process. Mickie and Alex had even gone to a movie premiere the night before, Billie had told him, and they'd been on the red carpet and in the press.

"Will he get out on bail pending trial?" Jason asked the lieutenant.

"I'm sure he will. Someone will pay it for him most likely. If he's found guilty, they could take everything he's got as restitution for the victims. His lawyer will try to make a deal if he pleads guilty." Jason wondered where Mickie would live in the meantime, if Alex's accounts were frozen. He might have set up a bank account for her, which would be frozen too.

When the meeting was over, he thanked the lieutenant and went back to his office. He didn't want to call Billie at work and tell her what had happened. There was too much evidence to tell her about. The lieutenant said that they'd probably get the warrant in the next two days, then there would be the arraignment the day after, and someone could bail Alex right after the arraignment. Jason knew that Billie would be shocked, and Mickie even more so, and she'd have to leave the house, maybe empty-handed if they didn't let her take her clothes. It shocked him to know that by the weekend Alex would be in jail, and then he would be out after the arraignment. The press storm was going to be enormous and Jason would be part of it, since he'd broken the story.

Jason met with Joe McCarthy that afternoon and filled him in, and Joe was in awe of the story. A high school dropout hairdresser had been practicing medicine on some of the most important people in L.A. for the last four years, and investors had put millions of dollars into his practice and toward his success. It was an incredible story. Jason wondered what would happen with the Korean investors. Their money would be seized as part of the profits of Alex's crimes. Jason couldn't imagine that anyone would stand by him. He wondered what Mickie's reaction would be and what she would do once the money was gone. The answer seemed obvious to him. He wondered if she would draw closer to Billie again, but he wasn't sure.

He trusted Billie completely, and he told her the result of the police investigation that night. She wasn't going to warn Alex or her sister. Mickie had made her position clear. But he thought Billie deserved to know the truth. She was shocked when he told her. It was a shocking story of perfidy and lies, and the incredible boldness of Addison treating patients and administering treatments he had no training to do. It was sociopathy to a very high degree. He was sure that psychiatric evaluation would be an important part of the testimony. It would be insane of Alex to go to trial. His story would make a fascinating movie.

Billie could hardly believe it either. She had been skeptical about him all along, but no one had thought it would be anything of this magnitude.

"In a way, they were perfect for each other," she said

sadly. "Mickie stops at nothing to get what she wants, and she's always had a very loose relationship with the truth. She lied about me constantly when we were kids, and everyone believed her. She's very convincing. I wonder if she'll stick by him now."

"Honor among thieves," Jason said, still stunned by everything Dan Kelly had told him. He was eager to know that Alex had been arrested and finally stopped. The game had to end here, and quickly, before others were injured. He thought of the brochure then, with the before and after photographs of Mickie that Billie had told him about. It was further proof of the fraud he had committed, telling people that Mickie was in her thirties when she was only nineteen and that her youthful look was the result of his treatments. Alex was a true sociopath, perhaps no longer even able to distinguish between truth and lies.

Jason hoped the judge would sign the warrant soon so the end of the story could begin to unravel, and he hoped that Billie wouldn't suffer too much for her sister, because it was sure that her sister wouldn't suffer for her. And Billie deserved justice now too. She had suffered at her sister's hands for too long. And this was the grand finale. He wondered where Mickie would go now and what she would do. Coming back to real life and a normal existence wouldn't be easy by any means.

Chapter 12

Billie was still asleep when her cellphone rang the next morning and she grabbed quickly to answer it, thinking that Alex might have been arrested, and Mickie was calling her for help. She had dreamt about her all night, and woken half a dozen times. Jason had pulled her close to him and held her, hoping to reassure her. She was afraid that somehow Mickie would be implicated and arrested too. It was not impossible, depending on how much she knew.

But the voice at the other end was unfamiliar and stirred a distant chord of memory, and as she came fully awake, Billie realized it was Charlotte Carter, her friend Tom's mother, calling. She wondered if she was in California calling to say hello, and then a ripple of fear ran through her as she sat straight up in bed. Jason was in the shower, getting ready for work.

"Mrs. Carter, are you okay?" Billie asked her kindly.

"Yes," she said in a small voice. "I got your number from your dad. I hope you don't mind."

"Of course not. Is everything okay?" There was silence at the other end, and she realized that Tom's mother was crying, and she didn't need to be told the reason why. There was only one reason why Charlotte Carter would call her. Tears sprang to Billie's eyes and she felt as though the air was being squeezed out of her, and she couldn't breathe.

"I know Tom would want me to call you," Charlotte said through her tears. "He was killed last night, somewhere in Syria. I don't think they told me where. I can't remember. They were on stealth maneuvers at night, to capture the home of a terrorist leader, and a land mine exploded. Tom was killed instantly. They said he didn't suffer," she said. "He died a hero's death." It seemed to comfort Charlotte, but it didn't comfort Billie. Tom had been her soulmate for twenty-one years, and still was, even though she hadn't seen him in a year and a half and hadn't known where he was.

"I'm so sorry," Billie said through her own tears. "I loved him so much. He was the best person in the world. He was the only friend I had growing up."

"I know, and I was so sorry when your mom died. She was a good person too. They're going to try to send what they can home when they clear the area. But they don't know when that will be. We're not going to have a funeral. We'll have a memorial service when we have him back. I just wanted you to know. I hope you're all right, Billie. If you come out this way, please come and visit us. We don't want to lose touch with you."

"Thank you, Mrs. Carter, you won't." Tom was twenty-four years old, Billie had just turned twenty-three. His parents were older than hers. They had had Tom in their mid-forties as a late surprise. And he was an only child. She knew that his parents were close to seventy by now. Her parents had been much younger.

"We always hoped you two would get married one day, when you grew up. You were such good friends."

Too good to want to ruin it with romance, so they never had. Romances didn't seem to last, friendship did. It seemed safer to both of them not to risk what they had. They had always agreed on that. He was like her brother and she was his soul sister. Now he was gone too. All the people she loved were being taken from her one by one. Her mother five years before, now Tom. Mickie had said she didn't want Billie in her life, and Billie believed her. Mickie didn't want or need anyone, except Alex, for his money and the opportunity he gave her, until she learned the truth. And her father didn't care about her, and never had. It made Jason even more precious, and she was pining for Tom when she and Charlotte hung up.

Jason saw her face when he came out of the shower with a towel wrapped around him. Her face was gray, she was so pale. Her eyes were huge and she was crying and couldn't speak or put down her phone. She was still holding it in her hand when Jason came and sat on the edge of the bed and held her.

"Was that your sister?" he asked, hating Mickie for the pain she caused Billie, and she shook her head, and couldn't speak through her tears for a minute.

"It was Tom's mother. My friend . . . Tom Carter, he was killed on a mission in Syria last night," she said, and choked on a sob again.

"I'm so sorry." Jason didn't know what to do to make her feel better. He went to the kitchen and brought her a cup of tea a few minutes later and she took it gratefully and sipped it, and set it down next to the bed.

He waited while she dressed and he drove her to work, and promised to call her later. She hadn't even been able to talk to Tom in the last year, but she thought of him all the time. And now he would just be a memory and she would never hear his voice again. The thought of it was nearly unbearable. Tom had been the only decent part of her childhood other than her mother.

She kissed Jason in front of the hospital, and jumped out of the Jeep. She told him she was okay when he called her at lunchtime, and she was in bed with her clothes on when he came home from work. She knew she just had to get through the days now until the pain was less acute, something she could live with. She had been through it with her mother, but she had forgotten how agonizing grief could be. Every memory she had of Tom was vivid. Every moment of their childhood came back to her. Every prank they played and the jokes they told, the trees they climbed, the streams they swam in, the cows they chased and horses they rode. The only prom they ever went to and she had to wear an old dress of her mother's because her father wouldn't buy her a new one, even though he bought a new dress for Mickie for prom every year, because she was the prom queen and beautiful. Her father thought Billie was small and insignificant and didn't matter. Tom told her she looked gorgeous in her mother's ugly dress. She remembered the times they got drunk together, the science homework she did for him and the essays he wrote for her. He would have been at her college graduation if he could have been, and she had been so proud of him when she saw him graduate from West Point. Every moment of their years together was sharply etched in her mind and on her heart. Never to be forgotten and forever loved.

Later that day, Joe McCarthy, the head of the crime section at the *L.A. Times* and Jason's boss, had called him to his office. Jason assumed he'd gotten more damning information on Alex Addison, and he went to Joe's office promptly after the call.

"More news?" Jason asked, slipping into the chair across the desk from his boss. "Did they get the warrant signed?"

"It'll take a couple of days." Joe smiled at him. "I've got good news and bad news. I just got a call from upstairs," which meant senior management.

"The police aren't dropping the case, are they?" Jason looked horrified.

"Definitely not. You've done a great job on this investigation. It's not over yet, and I'm sure you'll write a terrific piece on it. Prize-winning stuff." Jason was touched by what he said. "The bad news for me is it'll be your last piece for the crime section. They want you to follow this to the conclusion, but after that you're done."

"I'm being laid off?" Jason was shocked. He knew they were making cutbacks, but he hadn't expected them to include him.

"No," Joe said. "They're moving you to politics, and

kicking you up to senior reporter, with an office of your own. You could run that section one day, if Jack Bailey would ever retire." The head of the political section was the oldest department head at the paper, a famous old reporter with a column of his own. "They tried to steal you a year ago and I wouldn't let them, so my apologies if you stayed in the crime division longer than you wanted. You're a damn fine reporter, Jason. You've already done a great job with this investigation and we're just getting started."

Jason was stunned by the news of his transfer and the promotion. It was what he'd been dreaming of for three years. Joe said, "I think Addison will plead when he gets a deal and it'll wrap up pretty quickly. You'll be upstairs very soon. Congratulations!" He held out a hand and shook with Jason, who was ecstatic. He thanked Joe profusely and went back to his desk in a daze.

Jason told Billie about the promotion that night, and despite her grief over Tom, she was happy for him.

On Friday morning, Dan Kelly called Jason to tell him that Alex had been arrested and was in jail. He had been seeing patients when they came for him and took him out of the house in handcuffs, and his patients and staff had stared at him in silent disbelief. Kelly didn't say if Mickie had been there or how she'd reacted. Maybe she was out, shopping for some event.

The police were going to be searching the house and taking evidence with them. They had kept one office person to open the supply closet doors for them. They had to call a locksmith to open some of them, since only Alex had the combinations. They were sending all the substances to the police lab for analysis, since none of them were marked, and they would all be evidence.

Dan said that the arraignment was set for Monday, and exceptionally, the judge had refused to allow Alex to post bail until after the arraignment, so he would have to spend the weekend in jail. Jason wondered if Mickie was shocked, furious, or sympathetic. Mickie wasn't long on empathy at the best of times. She would be thinking of how Addison's fall from grace and exposure would affect her. His accounts had been frozen by the judge so Mickie would have to post bail herself, or someone else would. No one could pay his employees, unless the judge allowed money to be released from Alex's accounts to do so. But his medical office was closed forever. Dr. Alexander Addison IV no longer existed. His patients who were so dependent on him would be in a panic.

Joe McCarthy asked Jason to write the preliminary article that day for the headline on Saturday.

Billie couldn't stop herself, when Jason told her Addison had been arrested. She sent Mickie a text from the car on the way to work. It took her mind off Tom for a few minutes. She just said, "I'm thinking of you, call if you need me. Love, B." The response from Mickie was swift. "I don't need you, and never did. Did your boyfriend do this? If so, tell him to go fuck himself and you too. M." Billie knew from a lifetime of past history that Mickie was incapable of human kindness. She could only fake it if she wanted something. The rest of the time it was not in her skill set. She was everything Billie had always thought she was, completely narcissistic, a liar, and cruel. She wondered how Alex was showing up on Mickie's radar, as friend or foe, someone to love and support, or whether he had been erased off her radar the moment his bank accounts disappeared. Mickie had never said she loved him, nor had he said it to her. They weren't capable of it.

Jason's headline article about the rise and fall and arrest of Alexander Addison was an exquisite piece of journalism. There was no speculation, no guesswork, no judgment or ventured opinion, just straight, pure reporting of the highest order. The revelation that Alex was not a doctor, had never gone to Harvard or any med school and had no medical license, and the charges he was accused of, were the essence of the piece. It was an astounding article and when Billie read it, she was sure Alex's patients and most ardent supporters and investors in Bellissima would be in shock.

Roger Hodges had called his own lawyer for him and instructed him to post bail after the arraignment, to keep his wife happy, and Marilyn had gone to see Alex in jail in tears on Saturday afternoon. She and Alex had sat across from each other with the glass between them, speaking through a phone, and they both cried. She was surprised not to see Mickie there, and she wanted to know from Alex who had started this smear campaign against him, and he swore he didn't know.

Roger's lawyer had a different story when he called Roger to fill him in on the charges, explaining that five women had been disfigured by Alex's treatments and the substances he had injected into them, both counterfeit Botox and liquid silicone, which was illegal and potentially lethal, and possibly other unsuitable substances which remained to be seen. It was a sobering conversation, and it impressed Roger, along with the other charges, that Alex had been a fraud, a charming, brilliantly impressive one, who had pulled off an incredible scam. He was a hairdresser who began as a high school dropout, had been posing as a Harvard-trained plastic surgeon for years, and had gotten away with it. His luck had finally run out.

At Marilyn's insistence, Roger agreed to leave the bail

in place, but he was sobered by the charges. Addison was clearly a sociopath, not just a criminal. Marilyn said that Alex assured her that none of it was true. To keep peace in his already troubled household, Roger agreed to what his wife wanted, but his attorney told him that ultimately, Alex's only choice was to plead guilty. The evidence was too damning against him. And there was no doubt of his guilt.

Roger's attorney made the appearance with Alex at the arraignment where Alex pleaded not guilty, and bail was set at three hundred thousand dollars, which Roger paid. He knew that life with his wife would be unlivable unless he did. It was a small price to pay for peace, given her other justified grievances against him, including the girl in Newport Beach.

Jason attended the arraignment as part of his story, and with some misgivings, Billie went with him, in part so she would be there for Mickie if she wanted her. At first Mickie was nowhere to be seen in the courtroom, and then Billie spotted her, far from Alex and well behind him. Marilyn Hodges was in the front row, looking encouragingly at Alex, stoic in a black suit, shirt, and tie, as he pleaded not guilty. It was over very quickly once bail was set. He was returned to the jail until Marilyn paid the bail bondsman, and she was at the exit from the jail when he was released. She had also paid for a bungalow suite for him at the Beverly Hills Hotel. She had gone above and beyond for him with her total faith in him. And as he walked out of jail, looking badly shaken, he saw Mickie in the crowd behind Marilyn, waiting for him. He thanked Marilyn profusely, hugged her, promised to repay her as soon as things were straightened out, as he was sure they would be, then he walked toward Mickie waiting for him in the distance, as Marilyn left.

"I'm sorry," was all he could think of to say to Mickie when he stood in front of her. She didn't hug him as Marilyn had, but she was there. He had had no idea if he would ever see her again. She hadn't answered her cellphone when they let him call her.

"Now what?" was all she said to him.

"Where have you been?" he asked her.

"Where have I been?" she almost shrieked at him. "Not in jail." She had read Jason's article two days before, on Saturday. She didn't know what to say to Alex. He was a fraud. She didn't know what to believe now.

"Marilyn rented us a bungalow at the Beverly Hills Hotel. Can we go there and talk?" She nodded and he followed her outside to the car and driver she had hired to come to court. She had paid for it with her personal bank account, which had a few thousand dollars of her own in it, and some money Alex had given her. They seized everything that Alex owned and had frozen all his bank accounts. Alex looked respectable in his black suit, and he had a paper bag with his belongings in it. "Where did you stay last night?" he asked her again.

"Wendy let me stay at her place. We both cried all night. We didn't understand what had happened until we read the paper on Saturday."

"I thought you might have gone to your sister's," he said, very subdued as they got into the car.

"My sister and that creep she lives with are dead as far as I'm concerned. They started this. I'll never see her again."

"She didn't start it," Alex said quietly, as they rode to the hotel. "This isn't her fault. I knew it was coming and I didn't want to face it. I don't know how I got it, but I think I injected some bad Botox into some women a few months ago. It nearly killed them. They sent me registered letters and I ignored them. Five of them want to bring criminal charges against me. There may be more, and they'll sue me civilly. And we have a bigger problem." He looked at her and she could see that he was frightened. "We have to make a deal with the guys from Hong Kong. The Koreans are going to want their money back and we've spent a lot of it. The boat, the plane, some other things. I was happy to get their money, but I don't know how clean it is. They're kind of a rough group, and I think they may be in the drug trade.

I have to pay them back. We need the Hong Kong money to do that."

"And do what? You're not a doctor anymore. What are they going to pay us for? You were a hairdresser, Alex, and you *pretended* to be a doctor. Are you insane?"

"Maybe I am, or I was. But it worked for a long time. My patients love me. Maybe I can still do their Botox shots or some of the tamer treatments they rely on."

"Alex, if what the paper said is true, you're going to prison, and I'm not going with you. I'm getting out of this mess."

"Then why are you here now?"

"I don't know," she said as they reached the hotel. "Maybe I'm addicted to you. The police left me a message. They want to talk to me tomorrow. What am I supposed to say to them? I knew you did things you shouldn't have. I lied too. I just didn't know you're not a doctor. But they could charge me with fraud. I'm not going to prison for you." They had arrived at the hotel, checked in at the desk, and a bellboy showed them to their room. It was an adorable bungalow, with all the lavish comforts of the Beverly Hills Hotel and their own pool. The bungalow was costing Marilyn a fortune.

Alex poured himself a drink and sat down on the couch, and Mickie sat on the couch opposite and stared at him, feeling that she was in over her head. He drained the glass of Scotch and came over to sit next to her, and she didn't stop him. She half wanted to leave and half wanted to stay. She wanted to turn the clock back only days to when he was a doctor and he was rich, back to the yacht in the Caribbean and the plane. She didn't want to be tied to a criminal, or go to prison herself. She wanted a lawyer and didn't have one to call.

"I'm sorry," he whispered to her and kissed her, and the next thing she knew they were having wild passionate sex. They couldn't stop, and it felt like a death dance to her now. They made love until they couldn't breathe or move or talk, and then they fell asleep in a tangled mass of sheets.

Mickie woke up two hours later and went to take a shower. She was awake all night, thinking about him while he slept.

She had to go to the police. She wore the same clothes she'd worn to the arraignment the day before. All her clothes were at the house in Bel Air, which she and Alex had no access to now. She needed a lawyer to help her get out of this mess. Then she remembered that one of Alex's patients was an attorney whom Mickie had talked to several times while she waited for her Botox shots. She went to the living room of the suite, got the number from information, and called her. Her secretary came on the line and put her through to Patricia Scott. She sounded calm and kind on the phone.

"I was hoping you'd call me," she said smoothly. "Are you okay?"

"No," Mickie said, with a trembling voice.

"How's Alex? I saw the paper."

"He's a mess. And I swear I never knew."

"I figured. No one did. He's incredibly good at what he does. He probably believed it all himself after a while."

"I have to go to the police this morning. Will you come with me?" Patricia had a full calendar, but she wanted to help Mickie. She was young, innocent, and in a terrible situation.

"Yes, I will. I just have office appointments. I'll have my assistant cancel them. Where do I meet you?" Patricia wrote it down and thought of something she wanted to ask Mickie, now that some of the lies had been exposed. She was sure there were others. "How old are you really, Mickie?" Thirty-three had never rung true to her, even though Mickie was mature and dressed the part.

"I just turned twenty," Mickie said in a small voice.

"I thought it might be something like that. Let's get you out of this. Is there anything else I should know?"

"Not really." Mickie couldn't remember her own lies now, or even his. They had seemed true at the time.

"I'll see you at the police station in an hour. Don't start talking until I get there."

When Mickie got off the phone, Alex was awake. He looked as exhausted as she felt.

"Where are you going?"

"I told you, I have to talk to the police this morning. I just spoke with Patricia Scott. She's going to meet me there."

"She's a nice woman. I'm sorry, Mickie. This is such a mess. I never thought it would blow up like this."

"Yeah, neither did I." She realized now that she didn't love him. She never had. And he didn't love her. They had used each other and it got out of hand. She couldn't stand her sister, but she'd been right. Billie had sensed something off with Alex since the beginning. Mickie never had. All she could see were the diamonds in the sky, and she wanted to get them and grab them while she could. Alex had made it so easy to do that. She didn't care how many lies he told or how he bent the truth. He was doing the same thing she was. But she had never hurt anyone, and he had.

She wasn't sure that she would see him again. She didn't want to come back to the hotel. He was going to prison, and there might be a trial. It felt like this was the end. She wanted to get all her pretty clothes out of his house, but she didn't know how. Maybe Patricia Scott would help. Alex couldn't help her anymore. And what would they do

249

now until he went to prison? She wasn't an ambassador anymore. He wasn't a doctor. She hated to have Billie be right. She and Jason were so smug and so sure. Mickie didn't want to go crawling back to her. She had to figure out something for herself. At least she had the hundred thousand dollars in the bank that Alex had given her not to go back to school, when she lied about Stanford. It was all she had now.

She didn't feel guilty about lying to him. And she didn't feel sorry for him. She didn't feel anything except sorry for herself.

"The police took everything," he told her, looking bleak. "Will you stay at the hotel with me?" he asked her, looking tragic.

"I don't know," she said. "I don't know what to do now." She could go back to modeling, but she didn't want to. She had liked being with him, but she didn't like the way it ended, or what would happen now.

"What are you going to tell the police?"

"I don't know anything about the treatments you give your patients," she said to reassure him. "And I believed you were a doctor."

"Thank you. I'll walk you out," he offered. She had called an Uber and it was ten minutes away. She was going to ask the police if she could take her clothes out of Alex's house. He had bought most of them, but he had given them to her.

They walked side by side down the winding paths of the hotel grounds to the wide walkway at the entrance, and she stepped into the driveway. There was a white car with two men in it parked across from them, waiting for someone. Mickie thought it was her Uber, except for the man in the passenger seat, and as he opened the door and stepped out, Alex pushed her away, and the man came straight for him, shot him twice in the chest and once in the head, and jumped back in the car as Mickie stood in the driveway covered in blood. Alex lay in a pool of his own blood as people ran to him, someone screamed, and the car sped away. Nobody thought to stop it. They were all crowded around Alex and he was dead, with part of his head blown away and his chest wide open. Two people were holding Mickie up as she started to faint, and there was blood splashed all over her face and arms and in her hair. All she had seen were two men in the white car, and Alex had pushed her away as one started shooting, and then they were gone. They sat her down on the ground, and then she heard sirens. There were police everywhere and an ambulance came, and they put a tarp over Alex.

The police closed the entrance to the hotel, as it was a crime scene, and redirected people to the side entrance.

They led Mickie inside to a chair and gave her a glass of water. She was shaking all over, and they took her to a room to lie down.

Lieutenant Dan Kelly was waiting for Mickie when the sergeant at the reception desk came to tell him that her attorney was waiting outside at the front desk, and at the same moment he got a call on his emergency line. He closed his eyes and shook his head and told the sergeant to bring the lawyer in. He listened for a moment and spoke into the phone he was holding.

"I'll be there as soon as I can. Get the hotel video, names of witnesses. Keep the girl there. Is she hurt? Fine," Kelly said, and hung up as Patricia Scott walked into the room. She was a nice-looking businesslike woman in her fifties. She looked at him pleasantly.

"I'm sorry, Lieutenant. I didn't want to disturb you. I'm waiting for Michaela Banks. I'm her attorney, Patricia Scott." Kelly stood up to acknowledge her and sat down again.

"I'm afraid we have a situation. Apparently, Michaela Banks was at the Beverly Hills Hotel with Alex Addison. There was a shooting five minutes ago. Addison is dead. She's uninjured but in shock. She was standing next to him when he was killed. Two men in a car, one jumped out and shot him at close range in the head and chest, and they sped off. We've closed the entrance to the hotel, but they got away. It all happened very fast, execution style. We can see it on the hotel cameras. I'm afraid I need to go over there. Do you want to go with me and see Ms. Banks, or be there when she speaks to us?"

"Yes, I'd like that. The poor kid has been through a lot."

"Is she a kid?" he asked. "I was told she's in her mid-thirties."

"I believe Alex Addison told people that so they'd think he had worked miracles on her. She just turned twenty." She threw Alex under the bus for Mickie's sake. He was dead now anyway, so it didn't matter, and she wanted to play the youth card for Mickie. Dan Kelly groaned as he stood up.

"I have a daughter the same age," he said. "They get in one mess after another. They say she's pretty badly shaken up by the shooting." He led the way to the emergency door to the garage. A police driver was waiting for him, and he got in the front seat and directed Patricia Scott to the back seat. They took off in seconds, with the red light flashing and the siren on. They were at the hotel in six minutes, and the police on the scene conferred with Kelly for a moment. Alex's body was still on the ground covered by a tarp, an ambulance was waiting to take him to the morgue, and police were keeping bystanders away. They were putting up yellow tape to mark it as a crime scene. The press were arriving. A TV network news van had just appeared, and reporters would be there in minutes.

The manager led the lieutenant and Patricia Scott into the hotel after that. They had taken Mickie to a suite, and a police officer was handing her a glass of ginger ale to get some sugar into her. She looked very pale, and was still covered in blood. The officer retreated into the background when the lieutenant appeared, and Dan Kelly sat down across from Mickie.

"You've had a rough morning, Ms. Banks," he said sympathetically. "I'm sorry. I'm Lieutenant Kelly."

"He's dead, isn't he?" she asked.

"Yes, he is. Do you remember what happened?"

"I was waiting for an Uber, to come and see you. I spent the night here with Alex after he was arraigned. He walked me out. We walked into the driveway. There was a white car waiting with two men in it. I thought it was my Uber, but there were two men in the car. We were just standing there, and one man got out and shot Alex a bunch of times, maybe three or four. He jumped back in the car, and I don't remember, I was feeling kind of sick, I think they drove away."

"That sounds like a very accurate description. It's what

my men said too, and what the doorman reported. Did you recognize the men?"

"No. They just looked like regular men in a white car."

"Do you remember what they were wearing?" She thought about it, and seemed to calm down while she talked to him and sipped the ginger ale. Patricia Scott sat quietly, listening carefully.

"I didn't really see the driver. The one who shot Alex was wearing like a black baseball jacket, you know, zip up, maybe a black shirt and black pants. And he had a face mask on, like people wore during Covid."

"Short hair? Long hair?"

"Short."

"Anything else?"

"He had a gun. I think he had on blue or black running shoes." He sounded like a million other people on any street.

"Do you think you could talk a little about Alex now, and I can spare you a trip to my office?" She nodded. "Did he ever tell you or hint that he wasn't really a doctor?"

"Never. He told stories about his residency at Mass General, and med school at Harvard. And he acted like a doctor."

"Did he ever do treatments on you?"

"No, he said I was too young. He loved being a doctor. And he loved his patients." There was no expression on her face as she said it. Her face was still smeared with Alex's blood.

"Did he describe the treatments he did on them?"

"Not in any detail. Sometimes he'd say so-and-so is here for her Botox shot. But he never described the treatments, and I wasn't there when he gave treatments, only once or twice for easy stuff, like when they were waiting for the numbing cream to take effect for their Botox shots. He liked it when I talked to the patients in the waiting room to relax them and be friendly. He wanted me to go to parties with him, red carpet and that kind of thing. He said I was his 'ambassador,' but that's all I had to do."

"Did he pay you?"

"A little in the beginning. After that, he paid things for me. He paid me for the modeling at first, and a fee to be his ambassador. But eventually he just paid for my clothes."

"How did you meet him?"

"He hired me through my modeling agency to be in his ads when he was opening his center. He liked the way I looked so he used me as the face of Bellissima."

"Did you do a brochure for him too?" he asked her casually.

"I think so. I don't know. I never saw it."

He pulled it out of his suit jacket and handed it to her. "Have you seen that before?" She shook her head. He had grabbed it off his desk before leaving his office. He pointed to the before and after pictures. "Have you seen those two photos before? Can you describe them to me?"

"I've seen those photographs when we took them, but not together like that. The normal one he said was for the brochure. The other one was a joke, the photographer took it to show me what I'd look like when I'm old. He did it on his computer. I thought it was funny. I didn't think he would use it. It's really ugly." Dan Kelly and Patricia Scott exchanged a smile. Mickie's definitions of "really old" and "really ugly" were definitely a youthful point of view.

"Did he tell people you were older than you are?"

"Yes," she said.

"Did he tell you why?"

"He said he didn't want people to know he was dating someone my age. I was nineteen." Mickie knew exactly where she was going. It no longer mattered. Alex was dead. She was alive.

"When did you start dating him?"

"On the last day of the shoot for the brochure and ads. He wanted to take me out to celebrate how well it went. I went home, and he showed up at the apartment I shared with my sister. She graduated from college in May, and she came out here to be with me. She moved in with me. He came to the apartment and waited outside in his car.

He really wanted me to go to dinner with him, so I did. I didn't want to be rude or hurt his feelings. He'd been really nice during the shoot and paid me a lot. It took five days. We had dinner and he said he could really help with my career and introduce me to people, and movie producers, if I would go to parties with him and be seen with him, like a date. I'd been modeling here for a year, and waiting on tables since I finished high school. His was the best job I ever had. He paid me twenty thousand dollars for five days, through my agency. We had a lot of champagne at dinner and I got a little drunk, and he took me back to his place after dinner, instead of my apartment. And I think we had more champagne, I can't remember. I don't know what happened after that. He wanted to have sex with me, and I did. I think I passed out from the champagne, and he wanted me to do it again the next morning before he took me home. So I did." She looked momentarily embarrassed, as the lieutenant watched her closely. "I went home, and he came to our apartment again. He wanted me to go out with him.

"He invited me to a big movie premiere, and he kept saying he could help me, and I wouldn't have to wait on tables anymore, which sounded pretty good. I liked him. He was nice to me. At first, it was like we were dating, and then he wanted to have sex all the time, and he would tell me to go shopping and buy whatever I wanted. He liked me in sexy clothes. He wanted to have sex a lot, more and more, like five or six times a day, and he wanted me around so he could do that. He asked me to move in with him in October, and my sister had a boyfriend by then, and they were dating, so I wound up staying with Alex a lot, and it was easier just moving in with him. But once I moved in, he wanted to have sex all the time. He would come upstairs sometimes between patients and tell me to hurry up, or he would want to have sex with me all night long. Once I was living there, he wanted me to do weird kinky stuff, like tie him up, or hurt him, or put weird things up me, and I didn't know how to get out of it by then. He kind of made me his sex slave. It was embarrassing. He would tell me I could go shopping at Chanel if I let him do weird stuff to me." She hung her head in shame. "So I did. I never had clothes like that before and he let me buy whatever I wanted. Or he'd make me walk around naked all the time, or he'd come on my face, sorry . . ." She hung her head again. "He needed it all the time."

"Did he actually get you parts in a film or modeling jobs, like he promised?" Kelly asked her.

"No, he never did. He liked being in the press with me a lot, though, as long as I didn't tell people how old I was. I told him I wanted to go to college, and he paid me a hundred thousand dollars not to, so I could just be at the apartment, available to him. My sister was really freaked out about my being with him, but I didn't know how to get out of it, and I liked all the clothes I got. I never told her about all the sex."

"Where's your family, Michaela?" he asked her.

"My mother died six years ago, when I was fourteen. And my father is . . . well, he hasn't been okay since my mom died. He drinks all the time. I grew up in Iowa, we have a dairy farm. I left after high school. My mom was dead and my sister was away in college, and my dad was drunk all the time at night, so I left and came here to act and model. I did a lot of trade shows and waitressing. And then I met Alex. Before that, I had to do a lot of waitressing when I didn't make enough modeling. It was better when my sister moved out here last May after she graduated, so we could split the rent. I had two roommates before, but they left."

"Where did your sister graduate from?" He was just curious.

"MIT. She works at Cedars-Sinai. Her boyfriend is a reporter at the *L.A. Times*." And then it clicked for Dan Kelly that this was Jason Bell's girlfriend's sister he had referred to. It all made sense now.

"Do you remember meeting any Asian people with Alex, people who might have invested in his center?"

"Yes," she said clearly. "They were Korean. He told me it was a very important dinner. He took me. There were three men. They never spoke to me all evening, just among the men. I was kind of there for decoration. A few days later, he said they were giving him ten million dollars to open a center in Dallas. But he didn't do it. He leased a plane and we went on a two-week cruise on a yacht he chartered in the Caribbean for two million dollars. I think he spent some more of the money but I'm not sure. A couple of weeks ago we met with some people from Hong Kong, who were much nicer. They talked to me too. They wanted to invest twenty-five or thirty million dollars in a big beauty center in Hong Kong and they wanted Alex to create it for them, but I don't think they made the deal yet."

"I think the men who killed him today may have been sent by the Koreans, because of the money he spent, and that he got exposed as being a fraud and not a doctor," Kelly said. "It's just a theory, a possibility we'll explore along with some others. You've been very helpful, and I'm sorry you've gone through such an ordeal. There are some bad people out there, Michaela. You need to watch out for them." He said it to his daughter all the time. Then he turned to Patricia. "Ms. Scott, may I speak to you for a moment, and Michaela can rest for a minute? Thank you for speaking to me," he said kindly to Mickie, and left the room with Patricia Scott right behind him.

Patricia followed him outside the suite and they conferred in the hall. "The guy is lucky he's dead, he'd have a sex slave case on his hands. For God's sake, she's a kid off a farm in Iowa, and he had her prostituting herself for shopping while he made a sex slave of her. He's every parent's worst nightmare. I can't prove it yet, but I think his Korean associates got him for blowing their money and not delivering the goods, and turning out to be a fraud. And I'll bet you there was money laundering involved," Lieutenant Kelly said, looking irate at what Mickie had told them.

"Michaela wanted me to ask you if she can have her clothes from his apartment. She brought all the clothes she owned when she moved in, and everything he bought her is there," Patricia, her attorney, asked in a businesslike tone.

"She earned them. They were gifts to her, if you can call it that. Give me a time and I'll have two of my female police officers there and she can take everything that's hers. Everything else is going to be sold for the benefit of the women he damaged."

"In his defense," Patricia Scott said fairly, "I never knew that he was turning Michaela into a sex slave for shopping money, but I was a patient, and he was one of the best doctors I've ever gone to. He was amazing."

"He had the skill apparently, but not the training, the degree, or the license, and I don't think those five women would agree with you. But clearly, he was very convincing. A true sociopath."

Patricia wondered if all of Michaela's story was true. She had always looked very happy whenever Patricia saw her. But anything was possible. Some people appeared normal and had strange addictions, and apparently Alex Addison was one of them. Still, Patricia had always been pleased with her treatments. She was there to help Michaela get her things back, and get her through the interrogation, and she thought it had gone very well. Michaela had handled it masterfully. She had been open and straightforward and hopefully honest. And Alex was dead now. What Michaela said about their sex life would do him no harm. None of his nurses were bringing MeToo charges. Alex had been assassinated, and he had left five women disfigured for life. Michaela was getting to keep all her clothes. The lieutenant thanked her and went to talk to his men. And he was sure that Jason Bell was in the crowd of reporters outside. Patricia told Michaela that her wardrobe was safe. She did a little dance around to celebrate it, and looked like the kid she was. She didn't seem heartbroken over Alex's death, but if what she said was true, who could blame her. She was free now. Mickie said she wanted to pick up her clothes the next day.

The police told her she was free to go, and she booked a room at the Beverly Wilshire, on Rodeo, so she could shop to her heart's content until she figured out what to do next. She had Alex's hundred thousand dollars to coast on for a while. She thanked Patricia, took an Uber to the Beverly Wilshire, and checked in.

Dan Kelly called Jason when he got back to his office. The story was going to be on the news at six o'clock. There had been a bulletin on the one o'clock broadcast that there had been a fatal shooting at the Beverly Hills Hotel and one man was dead, but no further details were available at the time.

"I assume you were at the hotel."

"I was," Jason said.

"My personal guess is it's the Koreans he did business with. Apparently he was blowing their money, and when he got exposed as a fraud, they must have taken care of it. It's the most logical conclusion," Dan Kelly said. "And I spent almost two hours with Michaela Banks, who must be the person you mentioned to me earlier, your girlfriend's sister. The bastard turned her into a sex slave for shopping money. He was a piece of work. We're done with her. I'm going to let her keep all the clothes he bought her. The victims will get whatever assets he has split evenly among them. A judge has to approve it. But if he has no heirs, it won't be a problem. She had an attorney with her, oddly enough, a patient of Addison. And I hope Michaela has better luck and better judgment next time."

"So do we," Jason agreed.

"I'll keep you up-to-date on the details, so you can write the conclusion. He sounds like a sociopath to me," the lieutenant said, and hung up, and Jason reported the latest news to Billie when he called her.

"I think they were an even match," she said sadly about Alex and Mickie. "I think he may have been the sex slave, if I know my sister. She comes out smelling like a rose every time. Did she have an attorney with her?"

"Yes, apparently a patient of Alex's who agreed to help her. And she gets to keep everything he bought her. The rest will be sold for the benefit of the victims, since there won't be a court case now. His investors are the losers. It's an incredible story. It really is amazing that he pulled it off for as long as he did, and never had a mishap till now."

Jason wondered if Billie was right, if Michaela had tailored the story to her benefit, so she was the victim, and walked off with everything Addison gave her. Something told him that Billie was right. She knew her sister, and it rang true to Jason too. Even after seeing her lover murdered, she kept a cool head, and took care of herself.

Two officers met Michaela at the apartment the next day, and they used all of Alex's luggage to pack her extensive wardrobe. She had to get a van to take her back to the Beverly Wilshire. And she had taken the business card she wanted out of one of her evening bags. She remembered exactly where she had left it.

Chapter 13

The case against Alex Addison was closed very quickly. No identification was made of the man who had shot him or the getaway driver. There was nothing distinctive about them on the hotel security videos. They'd gotten a license plate, but it proved to be a stolen vehicle. So the murder case was dead. Alex died intestate, without heirs or a will, so all his possessions would be sold and added to the eleven million dollars he had in the bank. Each of the five women would get about three million dollars. It wasn't adequate compensation for their ruined faces, but it was something. All of them were satisfied that justice had been done, and no one shed any tears over Alex, except his most devoted patients and his staff. Mickie shed none, in her suite at the Beverly Wilshire, with a stack of Alex's luggage full of her clothes that she had retrieved from his home.

Billie texted Mickie several times to be sure she was all right, and she didn't respond. She had nothing to say to her. She didn't need an older sister anymore. She didn't need anyone except herself.

She had called the Hong Kong investors whose card she'd retrieved from the evening bag she had worn that night. The four men were still in L.A., doing business and meeting with companies they wanted to invest in. They told her they were sorry about Alex's untimely death, and didn't make a point of mentioning his exposure as a fraudulent doctor. It was a shocking and fascinating story that he had gotten away with it to the degree he had. He had incredible charisma and was amazingly bright.

Michaela told them when she spoke to them that she would still be interested in a job in their beauty center, or in one of their fashion investments. They had extensive ownership in several high-end shopping malls of luxury brands. They made an appointment to meet her at the Beverly Wilshire for a drink, to discuss it further with her.

They came with an open mind. She was honest with them about how old she was because she couldn't hide it from them if she wanted a job. She had written up a CV for them, including what her goals were. She thought it would be exciting to live and work in Hong Kong. She was interested in fashion and beauty, and they were impressed by how stylishly she was dressed. She would be a good representative of any of their brands.

Two weeks later, they offered her a position as a junior executive in marketing for their best shopping mall, and they were willing to groom her as a buyer. They would supply her an apartment in The Peak section of Hong Kong, with a starting salary of two hundred thousand dollars a year, which was high, but she was an unusual woman. She could start as soon as she was ready to leave, and she said she was. She said she had no family ties, and no reason to stay in L.A.

She called Patricia Scott after she accepted the offer, and asked if she was supposed to notify the police. As a courtesy, Patricia called Lieutenant Kelly and told him that Michaela had accepted a position out of the country in Hong Kong, and wanted to get a fresh start. He said he had no problem with it and she was free to leave. Patricia called Michaela and reported to her, and Mickie booked a ticket after that. She was ready for a new life.

Dan Kelly mentioned it to Jason the next time they spoke, that Michaela was leaving for Hong Kong and had taken a job there.

Jason told Billie about it that night, and she was surprised. "She's moving to Hong Kong? Why?"

"She got a job offer there, and maybe the whole mess with Addison burned her out. Seeing him murdered right in front of her must have been pretty awful. He would have gone to prison if he'd lived, probably for a long time. Maybe Hong Kong will be good for her." Billie listened quietly, and nodded.

She tried to call her again the next day, and texted her that she wished her well and would like to say goodbye.

"Why? We hate each other," was her response by text.

"I don't hate you. I love you. You're my sister," Billie said.

"I was switched at birth," Michaela answered.

"Me too. So what?" Billie persisted.

"I'm not like you. I don't need a family, or even want one," Michaela said. "I don't have feelings like you do. I don't need anyone." It was the most honest she had ever been with Billie. She had already called their father to say goodbye. He was surprised she was leaving and sounded sad. She told him her boyfriend had died and not the rest.

"Do you miss Alex?" Billie asked her, curious, still by text.

"No."

"When do you leave?"

"Tomorrow night."

"If you give me your flight number, I could say goodbye at the airport," Billie offered. She needed closure. Michaela didn't care.

She texted her flight number, and turned off her phone.

Billie told Jason the next day at breakfast that she was going to the airport to say goodbye to her sister.

"Did she say you could?" He was surprised.

"She texted her flight number, and I offered to say goodbye to her at the airport. Who knows when I'll see her again." Maybe never.

"That's how she wants it," he said gently. Billie was such a caregiver and so brimming over with love that she couldn't accept the fact that Michaela wasn't like her and was hollow inside. "I'll drive you," he volunteered. He wanted to be there for Billie. He was afraid it would be hard for her.

They got to the airport in plenty of time, put the Jeep in the garage, and walked into the international terminal. Billie looked for Mickie and didn't see her, and texted her.

"I'm here. Where are you?"

"In the first-class lounge." Mickie's new employers were paying for a first-class ticket for her. "I went through security early. You can see me from the observation deck when I go through to board the plane." Billie felt it like a blow. Mickie had put an airport and a glass wall between them, knowing Billie couldn't get through security without a ticket. She didn't want to be close to Billie and hug and kiss goodbye. She felt no emotion to be leaving her.

"Okay, I'll be watching for you from the observation

deck." Michaela wanted no personal contact, but their mother had left her in Billie's care. And if this was the best she could do, she was doing it. Billie had held up her side of the deal to the end. It was up to Michaela how much she wanted, and how much she could tolerate, how human she could be. Mickie didn't pretend to feel anything for her sister.

Billie was watching when the passengers started to board. She watched for her sister, but she didn't see her, and wondered if she'd missed her. Then she saw her, one of the last to board. Michaela looked stylish and grown-up in a black wool coat, tall boots, and a big tote bag for the long flight. Billie watched her, without taking her eyes off her, willing her to turn around. Michaela looked straight ahead, never looking up. She knew Billie was there. She was punishing her for the differences between them, for not understanding who she was. She didn't want to love or be loved. She and Alex had never told each other they loved each other, because they didn't. They had sex, they didn't make love. Love was too painful for Michaela. There was something missing inside her and she knew it. She didn't feel the things that other people did, or need them. Billie's shoulders sagged as she watched her sister. She could tell Mickie wasn't going to turn around. She would rather hurt Billie than please her. It was the eternal dance between the two sisters. One loving, and the other unable to love. Just like Alex, she was a sociopath, with a profound need to hurt others.

Michaela was just about to go through the last door to the plane when slowly she turned, and looked up. Their eyes met immediately, in spite of the distance. Michaela looked at her sister for a minute and never smiled. And Billie touched her heart. Even if she couldn't reciprocate it, Billie could send her a sister's love to do with as she chose. Michaela stood there and nodded. She acknowledged it, even if she couldn't send it back. She wasn't evil all the time. She was empty and she knew it, and Billie was brimming with love for her, and for Jason. She had loved their mother and would have loved their father if he had let her. Michaela took a last long look at her sister, and walked through the door to her new life, free from all her past lives and the people in them, as Billie stood watching the door until they closed it, and she saw the plane pull away from the gate and wished her sister well. She forgave her for all the pain Michaela had given her in their childhood, for all the mean things she'd done to her, for all the love she couldn't give and the things she had blamed her for.

She watched the plane take to the skies with her sister on it. The sister who didn't want to be one, the sister she had been, and the one Billie wished for and never had.

Jason gently put an arm around her shoulders. "Come on, let's go home," he said softly. Billie nodded and tucked herself under his arm. She felt liberated and lighter. She had finally understood and accepted who Michaela was.

She looked up at Jason and smiled. He kissed her. She was free now. Michaela couldn't hurt her anymore. Leaving her was Mickie's final gift to Billie, and the only way she knew how to love. They would be released now from the burden they had been to each other, and the pain it had caused. Billie had a good life ahead of her with people who knew how to love her and return the love she gave so generously. Michaela would have the life she chose, whatever she had to do to get it, just as she had always done, and knew how to do so perfectly, no matter what it cost, or who it injured, as long as she got what she wanted in the end. The only person Mickie loved was herself.

Jason kept a strong arm around Billie's shoulders as they walked out of the terminal together. They had a whole life to look forward to, as Michaela's plane disappeared, taking her to her new life, as far away from Billie as she could get, which was a blessing for them both. And all Billie could do for her now was wish her well.

Danielle Steel

Have you liked Danielle Steel on Facebook?

Be the first to know about Danielle's latest books,
access exclusive competitions and stay in touch
with news about Danielle.

www.facebook.com/DanielleSteelOfficial

THE COLOUR OF HOPE

A new beginning. A time to heal. A happy place.

After her husband's death, Los Angeles gallery owner Sabrina escapes to a beautiful château in France. Xavier, the owner of the château, is still reeling from the failure of his business during the pandemic, which dealt the final blow to his faltering marriage. As the pair inspire each other, Sabrina regains purpose by involving herself in the community and Xavier recognizes what he needs to do to step forward in both his professional and personal life . . .

ABOUT THE AUTHOR

DANIELLE STEEL has been hailed as one of the world's most popular authors, with a billion copies of her novels sold. Her many international bestsellers include *The Colour of Hope*, *The Portrait* and *For Richer for Poorer*. She is also the author of *His Bright Light*, the story of her son Nick Traina's life and death; *A Gift of Hope*, a memoir of her work with the homeless; and the children's books *Pretty Minnie in Paris* and *Pretty Minnie in Hollywood*. Danielle divides her time between Paris and her home in northern California.

daniellesteel.com
Facebook.com/DanielleSteelOfficial
Instagram: @officialdaniellesteel